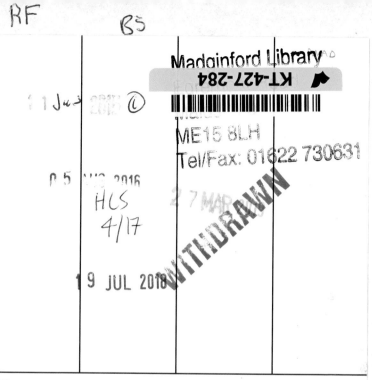

TANGO AT MIDNIGHT

Nicci Tate has to play the part of entrepreneur to persuade bank manager Grant Blake to agree a loan. This would make her dream of opening her own shop come true. However, Nicci has demons in her past which could jeopardise everything — including Grant's growing fondness for her — and she cannot let him get too close. But Grant, who has a problem with theft at the bank and his own dark mystery, isn't a man who's easily turned away.

CARA COOPER

TANGO AT MIDNIGHT

Complete and Unabridged

LINFORD
Leicester

First published in Great Britain in 2010

First Linford Edition
published 2011

British Library CIP Data

Cooper, Cara.
  Tango at midnight. - -
  (Linford romance library)
  1. Bank employees- -Fiction.
  2. Businesswomen- -Fiction.
  3. Love stories. 4. Large type books.
  I. Title II. Series
  823.9'2–dc22

  ISBN 978–1–4448–0794–3

Published by
F. A. Thorpe (Publishing)
Anstey, Leicestershire

Set by Words & Graphics Ltd.
Anstey, Leicestershire
Printed and bound in Great Britain by
T. J. International Ltd., Padstow, Cornwall

This book is printed on acid-free paper

1

Nicci Tate watched Grant Blake through the glass window. He looked every bit as scary as everyone said he was. Tall, imposing, square jawed and serious. She shifted uneasily on the smart leather seat and tried to wiggle her toes. Nothing doing. Her shoes were too high, her skirt too tight, her tailored jacket too fitted. This get-up just wasn't her. And yet, she knew this was what she had to do to get the money.

'That suit looks fabulous on you,' her friend Catherine Kincaid, known to all as Cat, had said. That was a week ago, when they had been in the changing room of Filmington's most expensive dress shop.

Nicci wrinkled her nose. 'Are you sure? Won't he just think I look too mutton-dressed-as-lamb?'

'No way. You look fab. Power dressing is what it's all about. We've got a week to make you look like a businesswoman. I know you love knocking about in jeans and t-shirts but that won't do for your meeting with Grant Blake. Bank managers expect people to look business-like. He always wears the sharpest suits, with knife-edge creases. You've got to exude success even before you've started your business. You have to make people believe in you, and most of all, you have to make Grant Blake believe in you.'

Nicci turned to look at the back of the suit in the changing room mirror. 'But the skirt's just too clingy. I feel all sort of exposed.'

Cat laughed. 'Rubbish. It's decent, it covers your knees. Look Nicci, I've worked at the bank for three years now. I've watched countless people going into Grant Blake's office asking for a loan to start up in business. Trust me, when people go to see him, they dress for effect. And that suit is seriously effective. Use what you've got — you're far too modest. You've got lovely blonde hair that you insist on bundling up in those rotten scrunchies, and shapely legs that never see the light of day. For once, play to the gallery. Here, these purple shoes will look terrific with the grey suit. Try them.'

'They are lovely,' Nicci squeezed her toes into the narrow points, 'but I'm not sure I can walk in them.'

'Sure you can girl, sashay over to that mirror and back again.'

Nicci tried and they were almost bearable. 'I suppose I can just about move. But they're not me.'

'You don't understand do you?' Cat pursed her lips, her face a picture of long-suffering patience. 'We don't want you to be you. You is that girl who's fantastic at cooking, who creates the most wonderful cupcake designs. You is that girl who only sells them from a teeny stall in the flower market at weekends despite everyone saying how terrific they are. You is that girl who's making just enough to keep her head above water and could do so much better. That's you. What we want to show him is the girl you want to be. The girl who's dreamt for years of setting up her own chic little shop with speciality teas and coffees with cupcakes to die for. The girl who will have so many orders coming in for weddings and corporate events that she'll be making a fortune. That's the you we want Grant Blake to see. And if you ask me, that's the girl who's standing in front of me right now with a drop-dead gorgeous figure and killer heels.'

Nicci turned to look in the mirror. Usually she never noticed how she looked. Baggy t-shirts were comfortable when you spent the day on your feet and up to your arms in flour and icing sugar. She didn't need to look smart. 'Perhaps you're right.'

'Sure am,' said Cat. 'Once we've got you a white shirt to tone it all down, a new hair cut and an ultra-smart briefcase to carry your business plan you'll be all set for your meeting next week. Grant Blake will be so keen to give you the money, he'll be offering you double.'

'I doubt it,' laughed Nicci, stepping out of the shoes and dropping back down to her normal five foot two inches. 'But thanks again for doing the business plan for me Cat. I could never have done it on my own, you know I'm simply rubbish with computers and anything to do with words.'

'Forget it. Just keep on supplying me with free cupcakes and I'll be happy. Maybe some time in the future, if I ever find a boyfriend who isn't a total loser, you'll be baking me a whole cake stand full for my wedding. You're not the only one to have dreams, you know.'

Nicci took her friend's hand. 'You'll find someone good enough for you if you try. Perhaps we'll both see our dreams come true, one day.'

As Nicci sat in the chrome and glass reception area waiting to go in to see

Grant Blake, remembering Cat's words made her smile. Cat was the best friend she'd ever had. Solid, dependable, fun, warm, always there for her. They balanced each other perfectly and had helped one another through many a crisis. Nicci thought about how kind and helpful Cat had been and suddenly a blush of embarrassment flooded Nicci's cheeks.

The secret Nicci had never told Cat, the thing she kept hidden from Cat and everyone else made her feel as low as a rat. The secret gnawed at Nicci. She kept it well hidden but always felt one day she would be exposed, embarrassed, found out, laughed at. But no one must ever know. Not Cat, not any of her friends and certainly not Grant Blake.

Suddenly Nicci's hands started to sweat. She could see the Bank Manager lean his tall frame over his desk and shake hands with the gentleman who had been in before her. The man had a smile on his face. His loan had obviously been approved. It was her turn now.

She swallowed hard, took out her handbag mirror and checked her appearance. Her blonde hair had been cut into a sleek long bob to frame her face. She wasn't used to wearing makeup but Cat had insisted on giving her the works. Mascara made her blue eyes bigger and a lick of plum-coloured lipstick made her lips look plumper. Oh yes, she had her war paint on all right. Thank heavens because, as Grant Blake got up, she could see he was imposing, over six foot tall with the build of an athlete; wide shoulders and powerful chest under his smart suit and pale green shirt.

Grant Blake ushered his previous client out and said without smiling, 'Miss Tate, come in please.' Nicci plastered on a convincing smile and tried to display confidence in her stride. As she walked into his office, her insides turned to spaghetti as the glass door closed behind her.

* * *

Grant motioned her to a chair. The ebony desk was huge, like a desert between them. She felt tiny sitting opposite his commanding frame which blocked out the light from the window behind.

'Coffee?' he asked. She didn't want one, but her mouth was so dry she wouldn't be able to talk without one.

'Thank you,' her voice sounded small in answer to his resonant tones.

She'd imagined he would call a secretary to bring in the coffee. This was a large branch of the bank, serving the market town of Filmington as well as half a dozen surrounding villages. Grant was an important man, making decisions on the finances of local farmers, builders, and countless other small and large businesses. But instead of calling for a secretary, he got up, and walked over to a jug where brewed coffee was steaming in the corner. As he filled two plain white porcelain cups, it gave her a chance to study him more closely.

In profile, he had a Roman nose, stately and studious with a kink in it which made her think he had broken it at some stage. She figured he might have been a rugby player in his school days; his shoulders were broad enough. He had a smooth, assured way of walking. As he placed the cups on the desk and settled back into his chair, she saw him raise a hand to the back of his neck and knead it; a sure sign of stress. She guessed this whole process was hard work. She must be one of a long line of hopefuls who'd traipsed through his office this morning.

Instantly her spirits dropped. What if he'd had enough of talking to people about loans today? Grant Blake had already given the man before her what he wanted, perhaps that meant he'd find it easier to turn her down. How many people had trouped through this door clutching their business plans? It may have been a daily occurrence to him but for her this was life changing. Obtaining a loan meant everything to her. She had dreamed of buying a shop, a proper business, something she could shine at for once. And sitting opposite her was the man who could wave a magic wand to make it happen or show her the door, crushing her ambitions to dust.

Grant Blake stirred his coffee deliberately. This was much more difficult than she'd imagined. In any other circumstance she'd have found him good looking. Broody, it was true, but a man you'd look twice at. The serious grey eyes gave away nothing as he raised them to her. She realised she'd been so mesmerised by his looks, she was staring and forced a nervous smile.

'So, Miss . . . '

He'd forgotten her name. 'Tate,' she provided.

'Yes, Miss Tate.' He shuffled the papers in front of him, bringing her business plan to the top. 'What can I do for you today?'

Give me some money, please, just enough to start up a little cake shop. 'Well, I have a business proposition to put to you.' She began, remembering the lines she'd gone over in her head a thousand times. 'You have my business plan in front of you.'

She put her briefcase, which she'd been clutching on her lap, down on the desk and undid the catches while she talked, ready to take out the document and refer to it. As she looked through the pockets of the briefcase trying not to look as terrified as she felt she said, 'I have a copy of it somewhere here. On page two there's my basic proposal and on page three my existing experience, while on page eight I've detailed my existing accounts for the business I've been doing at my market stall over the past two years . . . ' She stopped in her tracks; the pocket of the briefcase which should have held her neatly typed business plan was empty. Her fingers flipped from one pocket to another. Where was it? She froze, her blood turned to ice and she couldn't feel her feet. The paperwork was going to be her prop, something to hang on to, to stop her fidgeting and looking foolish.

She had been going to sit back, look relaxed and wax lyrical about each page in turn. It wasn't that she needed to have it in her hand — she knew the proposal off by heart, page numbers and all — but she was so convinced she had to have her paperwork with her to look professional. And of all the unprofessional, foolish, idiotic things she could have done. Disaster had struck. She'd gone and forgotten it.

2

She snapped the lid of the briefcase shut, hot and cold waves of anxiety flooding over her. She had one more thing inside her briefcase that she hoped would clinch the deal. A box of her novelty cupcakes, twenty-four of them tied with a pretty green and yellow ribbon. But now they seemed so stupid and girly and childish that she blushed to think of it.

Her presentation wasn't going anything like she'd imagined. She couldn't possibly bring out that silly looking box and place it on this huge official looking desk. Gulping she looked up, sure he would have found her out. A man as astute as him must have realised she was a sham and had forgotten her precious document. He'd be sure to show her the door.

He was leafing through his copy of

the business plan, the one she had posted him when she'd been granted an interview. His face was unreadable. The expression, if anything hard. If only the floor could open up now with a huge wide crack that her chair could simply collapse into like a tank rolling onto quicksand she would have been relieved. She so did not want to be here making an utter fool of herself.

'This figure,' he placed one well manicured finger onto the sheet in front of him which Cat had so carefully typed for her, 'of your takings for last year. Are you telling me, Miss Tate, that these takings are just from two days a week of running your market stall?' Did he sound as if he didn't believe it or was that just her over-anxious imagination?

'Just two days, that's right,' she grabbed her coffee gulping some down. She had to hold it with two hands, they were shaking so much. Nerves made her throat like sandpaper, her mouth like the inside of a spin dryer.

He was going to pick holes in

everything; tell her that her projections were rubbish and based on fantasy. She leapt in to put him right before he even started. 'I only run my stall at the weekends, at the markets in Dewkesbury on a Saturday and Filmington on a Sunday. They're the biggest markets and I spend all week making my cakes. I've doubled my output in two years. By the end of the day, they've always gone, earlier than the end in fact. I could probably sell twice as many, maybe three times, if I had a shop.'

She was aware she was gabbling and promptly shut her mouth. Besides, she hadn't breathed in what seemed like ages.

'Cupcakes.' He said it flatly. Was that scorn in his voice or was she reading too much into his every word?

'Yes.' Hastily, she clunked her empty cup on its saucer and lifted the lid of the briefcase again. She may have forgotten her business plan, but she had brought some photographs, in a neat album. She pushed it to him. She mustn't babble again like a woman possessed but she could feel her enthusiasm overflowing as it always did when she talked about her work. She flipped open the front page of the album which lay upside down to her and pointed. 'I iced those cakes with tiny squirts of green icing to look like grass and then did individual daisies and violets and dandelions in the centre of each one. They were for a party marking the opening of a local garden centre. They absolutely loved them and I think I got as many orders for cupcakes as they did for plants that day.

'And here,' she flipped the page, 'these cupcakes iced in baby pink and blue with tiny rattles and little marzipan teddy bears were for a christening. The customer had twins — it was a lovely job to do. She also hired two of my large cake stands and I had to do 70 blue cakes and 70 pink cakes so that each of the 70 guests could have one of each. They made a beautiful display, particularly when I linked the stands together with blue and pink satin ribbons and hung iced pairs of pink and blue bootees from the ribbons. The customer was thrilled.

'And these ones were lovely to do.' Nicci was finding it difficult to stretch over the big desk so she stood up and leant over it. 'See, they were for a fifth birthday. The mother had taken her little girl and her friends to the zoo for a party, so I made iced animals — lions, tigers, monkeys, elephants, meerkats — and placed one in the centre of each cake. The giraffe was the most difficult one, in the end I gave up with him because his neck got in the way of the lid of the box and I couldn't figure out a way to package him without his neck breaking. The children loved them so much, half of them didn't eat the animals but kept them in their party bags to take home and show their mothers. That was one of the best compliments I've ever had.'

Nicci's feet began to pinch as she

stood up leaning over in the high shoes, so she sat on the desk, twisting around, desperate to explain her ideas to Grant Blake, not seeing his eyebrow raise as she sprawled in his direction. 'This was a brilliant job to do,' she said, totally absorbed in her photo album, elbow leaning on the desk, undoing her tight jacket absent mindedly so she could lean forward and point out the cakes to him. 'They were for a little boy's eighth birthday. He was keen on Marvel comics and I loved doing Spiderman, Superman and Cat Woman. A friend got the pictures off the internet. The little boy and his friends loved them.'

As Nicci looked up, she realised with horror she had got totally carried away. The smart and in control business-woman she had wanted to be had given way to an over-enthusiastic anything-but-cool girl who had taken over his desk and was almost lying across it, gabbling away like she was chatting to one of her friends! Embarrassed, Nicci shimmied off the table, buttoned up her jacket and plonked back into her chair. 'Well, um . . . ' she said, feeling her throat go dry again, 'Those are my ideas anyway.'

He breathed in and steepled his hands thoughtfully, the picture of calm opposite her lively enthusiasm. 'So, you are already taking commissions.'

'Yes, but I could take more. If only I had a shop front to advertise my wares and put up photographs.'

'Couldn't a website do that for you?'

'Yes, I've thought of that. And my friend is already doing one for me.' Nicci was careful not to mention that Cat, who worked in the same bank, was her friend. Best keep this on the level. After all, Grant Blake was Cat's boss and Nicci wasn't trying to get her loan in any unfair way. In return for Cat doing the website, Nicci was going to make a grand box of cupcakes for Cat to give to her mother on Mother's Day.

'Websites are all very well, but most of my business is local. I haven't yet got into posting out my cakes through a delivery system, although I think I could in time. I'd have to investigate boxes and packaging to keep them secure in the post. I'm aware of not stretching myself too much. After all, I am a one man band — or rather one woman band, if you get my drift. If I had a shop front to display the prices and do seasonal displays to catch the eye I know I'd get more orders and they would be local and easy to deliver.'

'You've thought all this out haven't you?'

'Endlessly,' she stated. And she had. Whenever she had thought about the awful secret which blighted her life, she had turned to her cakes for solace. They were such positive things. They helped her forget the huge problem that weighed her down. The cake business had been her salvation. Cakes were tasty, celebratory, welcoming, they brought a smile to people's faces. Or at least most people, even though Grant Blake hardly ever seemed to smile.

Perhaps, Nicci thought in that

moment, perhaps she should bring out
the cakes she had brought with her. She
decided she had totally blown this
interview anyway by looking like a
chirpy, naive schoolgirl, sitting herself
ridiculously on the bank manager's
desk. She had wanted to look like a
level headed twenty-five year old
entrepreneur but she had blown that.
Oh well, she thought, nothing to lose
now. She couldn't look any more stupid
than she already had.

'Anyway,' she stated, reaching into
her briefcase and bringing out the box
tied with ribbon. 'I thought I ought to
bring some of my product with me for
you to try. Even if you don't give me
the loan.' She looked at him pointedly.
He glowered back at her, giving nothing
away.

She placed the box on the table. It
looked beautiful. It was a gold box, with
scalloped edges. One of the new ones
she had sourced from France, expensive
but worth it for special orders.

Grant looked deeply sceptical as she

pushed it towards him and motioned for him to open it. He undid the carefully tied ribbon and she noted, despite herself, that he had no wedding ring on his finger. Nicci held her breath as he lifted the lid. Maybe there would be something in there that would melt his ice cold exterior. As she looked, she was delighted to see just a twinge of approval cross his features.

'May I take one?' he asked.

'Of course. They're for you. Not a bribe, though,' she volunteered a joke, giggling, but then stopped and tried to be serious. Grant Blake didn't seem to do jokes. 'But no, of course they're for you and the staff to try. I did twenty-four cakes — I hope that's enough.'

'They're very clever.' He held the intricately iced cake in his hand examining it under the bright office lights. Then peered in the box to look at the rest. She had carefully iced each one with symbols and items that had to do with money. Pound signs, dollar signs, coins, and on some, carefully crafted fifty pound notes which had taken her ages to draw in icing by hand. All the cake bases were chocolate because chocolate was everyone's favourite flavour.

'The insides are full of my own chocolate truffle sauce,' she said. 'It's a smooth, velvety ganache of plain chocolate, sugar syrup and rich double cream.' She waited while Grant placed one in his mouth. His lips were beautifully shaped, with a row of neat, perfectly even white teeth. Slowly he savoured the dark chocolate and the sponge which was light as air.

'Good?' she asked anxiously.

'Very good,' he pronounced.

'Then, would you, could you, give me the loan?' It was so forward of her, she surprised herself. But then, she was sure he wouldn't give her the money, so sure she hadn't been reserved or cool enough to be seen as a good investment. Nicci held her breath. Again he flipped through the business plan, a frown developing between his eyebrows. That was it. That frown said everything. The money wasn't hers. She might as well pack her things now, get up and tottle out on her ridiculously high heels.

He closed her business plan and put it down on the desk. He took his hands and steepled them in front of him, resting his chin on their tips.

'Miss Tate,' at least he'd remembered her name this time. 'I have to admit that when I saw an entire proposal based on cupcakes I was sceptical. I used to like cupcakes as a child but I've never seen them as sophisticated or worthy of turning into an entire company. But you've done well, very well. You've turned one basic product into many products with all your different designs. They are fantastically well executed and you are to be congratulated.'

But. Nicci could feel a big 'but' behind all his words. He was building up to say no, she was sure of it. She had done something fundamentally wrong.

Maybe he'd seen through her. He was obviously a very able man. Maybe somehow he'd discovered her secret, realised she was a fraud. How she had no idea. Nobody knew she was a fraud although that's what she was. She blushed, turning bright pink.

'But.' Here it came. She wanted to run right now. 'Although I'd very much like to, I cannot lend you the money right now.'

Was that a yes or a no? 'I don't understand,' she stammered.

'I would like to lend you the money. You've brought one of the best business propositions I've seen in years. Your presentation was, uh . . . ' He leant back in his chair, and looked at the ceiling, searching for the words, ' . . . somewhat unconventional, but striking in its own peculiar way. Usually my clients stay in their seats, they do not go hiking over the furniture.' Nicci's blush flamed right to the top of her head. 'But I'm refreshed by your enthusiasm, your commitment and your drive. They're essential entrepreneur qualities. But you are unlucky in one respect, and that's why I cannot yet lend you the money you're asking for.'

'What do you mean?'

'Because I have already allocated the funds at present available. I'm sorry, I know that's not what you want to hear. But being in my position, I hold regular interviews for local business people such as yourself and always, a proportion of the ideas are not workable. I always have to turn people down. Unfortunately for you, this set of interviews have been extraordinarily productive. There have been some excellent proposals which in all fairness, I could not turn down. You see, the bank does not have unlimited funds. I only have so much in the pot, so to speak.'

'Then if the pot was empty, why did you still agree to see me?' Nicci was feeling not a little peeved. Had she come here for nothing?

'The law of averages dictates that, in

a morning like this I turn down about 50 per cent of the people I see. But today has been different. It's just life I'm afraid Miss Tate. There's a queue and you were unfortunate enough to be at the back of it. You're my last appointment today and you were behind other clients who had good ideas and whose loans I approved.'

Nicci felt like a balloon leaking air. Deflated, all her hopes died at his words. He had no money to give her and her shop would never happen. Obviously her feelings were written across her face.

Hastily, he leant forward. 'That doesn't mean to say I won't have more funds in due course. I just can't promise it.'

'I'm sorry. I'm very confused.'

For once, Grant Blake raised the glimmer of a smile. 'What I'm trying to do is, not put your hopes up, but to tell you honestly that there may well be the possibility of a loan in the future.'

'There may?' Nicci could feel her

balloon inflating again.

'Yes. I just can't promise it and I can't say when. These are difficult economic times. A credit crunch is exactly that. Credit is difficult to come by. But oddly enough, straitened economic times often produce outstanding entrepreneurs like yourself and I'd like to help if I can — when I can.'

'What does that mean in practical terms?'

'You're a very direct woman. I admire that. It means I'll contact you if and when I get extra funds that I can allocate. In other words if a loan becomes possible, I'll call.'

'Thank you. Thank you so much.'

'Don't thank me too much. I don't know when I might be in touch, it could be a long time and things may have changed by then.'

'But you've got my number?'

'I've got your number. And remember, there might be a cash freeze on for some time.'

'I understand.' Nicci got up, unable to stop the smile beaming across her face. 'Please, keep the cupcakes. My gift.'

Grant rose up to his full height, came around the desk and offered his hand. He had a firm grip that engulfed hers. As they stood, Nicci bathing in the warmth of knowing her dream was one step closer to coming true, she had the insane urge to hug Grant. He was an attractive man. What's more, now she was closer, she could feel the warmth emanating from his purely masculine body. Many years trying different tastes for her cupcakes had made her acutely aware and appreciative of scents, and her nose crinkled as his classy after-shave of lime and sandalwood tingled her senses. The urge to grab him in a hug almost overcame her, but she checked her natural exuberance — she didn't want him to think she was crazy. She got the distinct feeling the Ice Man wasn't used to hugs. She simply held on to his hand, wanting to express her thanks, until he pulled gently away.

She left his office, walking on air. Her friend Cat who had been away from the counter when Nicci had arrived for her appointment was now there, serving a customer. Cat glanced up, an anxiously questioning look across her face. As Nicci walked by, she smiled and winked. They had agreed to meet in an hour for lunch and she would tell Cat all about it then.

As Nicci stood outside, the spring sunshine warming her face, she only had one doubt. Would she get the loan she so desperately wanted before Grant Blake found out her appalling secret? For, if he did somehow get to learn the thing she hid from everybody there was absolutely no chance he would let her loose with all that money. Head suddenly bowed in thought, Nicci made her way down the street to the coffee bar to wait for Cat to come and meet her.

★　★　★

As Grant Blake peered out of the half shut blinds of his office, he was desperate to see Nicci Tate walk by. There she went, head held low. Why did she look so grim? He hoped he hadn't been too heavy on the negative side. He'd wanted to be honest and not raise her hopes in case there was a loan freeze. What he couldn't say was that she would definitely be on his list as soon as the funds came through.

He craned his neck, hiding behind the blinds, desperate to watch her every step. As she walked by, he allowed himself a rare smile to think how uncomfortable she'd seemed in her woman-of-the-world tailored suit. She'd looked fantastic but it was clear to him that playing the go-getter wasn't normal for her. He wondered what she would have looked like in her civvies, no makeup, weekend clothes, relaxed.

He'd probably never get to see that, he thought with a pang. But boy, was she fun. Fun — that was something that didn't often enter the world of Grant

Blake. His world consisted of spread-sheets, balance sheets, cold facts and monthly figures, not kooky girls who were so galvanised by their ideas that they forgot themselves completely and virtually crawled over his desk to show him how excited they were with their own innovations.

She truly was an exceptional young woman. My goodness, if he'd had her on his sales team for new financial products, his branch of the bank would be the highest earner in the country. The extraordinary thing was she was so obviously oblivious to her own talents.

And, he mused, brows knitted in thought, oblivious to her own beauty. Now that was an unusual thing. Only once before in the whole of his thirty years had he ever encountered a woman who positively glowed in the way that Nicci Tate did. It was when he was a teenager and his parents had taken him to see a new production on the London stage. They were lucky to get tickets. Everybody had been talking about the luminous young actress who had stolen the hearts of everybody who saw her, making the production an instant hit.

Grant's mother had always been star struck and regularly performed amateur dramatics in a local group. So, when the show had finished, she had insisted they wait out in the cold with a small group of strangers, dedicated theatregoers, to seek autographs. After about half an hour, the young actress had finally arrived — scrubbed of her make up, her hair newly washed and loose, Grant had never seen any woman looking so gorgeous.

Until today that was. The day Grant had seen the young actress, he had fallen in love. But of course that was a simple adoration because, apart from her signing his autograph book with her bold sweeping hand, he never saw the actress in the flesh again. He worshipped and loved her from afar keeping every cutting of all her many shows and films, until she finally married and disappeared from the limelight. He had been in love with her in a puppyish teenage way. But he had never been in love with a real woman.

Grant Blake was too practical for that, too down to earth, too centred on his career. What's more, he would never marry and have kids. Others might see him as solid and responsible but in his heart of hearts, he knew differently. He knew he had a weakness and that he'd failed all those years ago. And for that reason, he had steered clear of all real relationships and concentrated on his work. Work was safe. He was good at work. Admired and trusted. What woman could trust him after what he had done in the past — after he had failed so dismally and ruined so many peoples' lives?

The small smile Grant had allowed himself while thinking of Nicci Tate was wiped off his face at thoughts of the past. Forget it, he told himself for the millionth time, knowing that he never could and that in an unguarded moment he would remember again.

As he put the coffee cups on the side to be collected by his secretary, Grant's hand settled on the little lipstick imprint left by Nicci Tate and he stared at the plum-coloured stain left on his thumb. The spring sun drifted through the window illuminating the colour and making the tiny sparkles of lipstick glitter like sun on a fast running stream. Purple shoes, purple lipstick, she had tried so hard.

Grant took out his perfectly laundered handkerchief and reluctantly wiped the stain away. His thumb looked clean again, but dull and lifeless. He sighed, thinking of so many things that would never be. It was so much easier for him to focus on work. After all, he had a massive problem on his hands, a strong suspicion that one of his staff was committing fraud and it was his unpleasant task to find out who.

3

Cat pounced the second she walked through the door. 'How did it go? I've been desperate to know! You had a funny expression on your face when you walked out. Was he nice to you? What did he say?'

'Goodness Cat, take a pause for breath!' Nicci laughed and moved aside her briefcase so Cat could put her tray down. Pret was their favourite haunt for eating after work. Lots of wide squishy leather sofas and the most delectable ciabatta sandwiches. Cat tucked into her favourite mozzarella, smoked ham and mustard, toasted and warm just the way she liked it. While Nicci was trying one of their blueberry muffins. She had considered adding muffins to her repertoire but they didn't afford nearly as much vent to her creative spirit as an iced cupcake did.

'He was okay.' Nicci said.

'Just okay?'

'Well, you know what he's like better than I do. It's difficult to know what he's thinking. He lets you do the talking and before you know it, you've laid all your cards on the table and he hasn't even shown his hand.'

'Tell me about it. He does my supervision and appraisals.' Cat wiped a stray drip of mustard from the side of her mouth. 'He's nice enough, very fair, but you're right, there's a sort of holding back about Grant that none of us at the bank have broken through. Some of the girls really fancy him, but they think he's a bit unhappy. He has this incredibly serious mask that he never lets slip, even at the Christmas party he hardly lets go, whereas most of us are close to dancing on the tables.

'Anyway, enough of Grant Blake, the most important thing is, did he give you your loan? Please say he did. I'm so desperate to get in and help you do up that shop, it would be so perfect for you.'

The shop was below Nicci's flat, at the beginning of the famous flower market at Filmington. Filmington was a busy, bustling town at the best of times but it really came into its own on market day. Nicci had been brought up in the flat above the shop which had been a dry and dusty hardware shop. The couple who had run it, Mr and Mrs Hope, had finally decided it was time to retire. They had moved down to the sea and were keen for Nicci to buy it. They'd known her since she was a child and had seen all the problems she'd had to put up with from her parents. In some ways they had been like surrogate parents to her when her own were too wrapped up in their own problems to help her.

Mr Hope had confided to Nicci the day he had put the shop up for sale. 'It needs a load doing to it, a complete re-fit I'd say. We haven't maintained it over the last ten years. There's damp coming in at the back but it's only where the drain pipe needs fixing.

'Sybil and I didn't have any enthusiasm left for the place. But it's a great little shop and you could really do something with the area out the back. We've only ever used it for storing all the gardening stuff we used to sell, compost, pots and the like. But it's got a nice solid wall around it and if you carted out all the old stones and rubble in the corner you could lay a wonderful patio out there.

'I wish we could give it to you, Nicci, but selling that shop is going to fund our retirement. The only thing is, love, if you can get something of a loan, we'd be ready to negotiate downwards. If only we could come back and visit at some point and see you settled with a thriving little business. Well, that would make our retirement complete.' He paused, his eyes misting over. 'You know we always felt for you, with your parents the way they were. You had a lot to deal with from very young. Maybe now you're going into a new phase so to speak. The shop could be the making of you.'

Mr and Mrs Hope had always been so good to her. Sometimes she felt they were the only ones who really knew what she had to put up with. It had started soon after Nicci had begun school. Her father had had an accident on a building site where he was working. After a long time off work, he had started to turn to food for comfort and had eaten too much and sat around too long. Her mother had been a dinner lady. She'd always been overweight and gave up her work to look after him. But instead, she indulged him with cakes and home made bread, just making him worse rather than better.

Both of them had spent most of the day watching television and it wasn't long before being so large had told on their health. They both ended up with diabetes, giving them terrible problems with their eyesight and their legs. Gradually, as Nicci grew older, she became the person who cared for them. She would have to do the shopping and the cleaning and run errands.

Whenever one of them was ill, which became more frequent, Nicci had to stay off school. Her mother would write her sick notes saying, 'It's just this once Nicci. You are a good girl looking after your old mum and dad like this. We would try and go out but those stairs are such a killer. Anyway, if you stay home, you can watch telly with us. We'll be all cosy won't we?'

But Nicci's days off became more frequent and even when she did go back to school, she had missed so much she never caught up. She found that by being quiet and shrinking to the back of the classroom she could get away without being noticed.

Nicci had always hoped that one day her parents would get better and start to go out and about like the other mums and dads. But it was never to happen, and the flat became their world. From their upstairs kitchen window, they would have large comforting fried breakfasts and watch the people coming and going, especially on market day. The year before the Hopes moved out, Nicci's parents had finally succumbed to years of over-indulgence. First her father died of a heart attack then her mother shortly afterwards. It seemed to Nicci they had only held on for each other. It had broken her heart to think how much of their lives they had wasted, and made her determined not to waste her own.

Nicci had inherited the flat, but it was eerily quiet without them. The only way Nicci knew to ease the grief was to get rid of a lot of the clutter, completely repaint and, with the tiny bit of money she had saved, get the kitchen re-fitted. For her, the kitchen, where she created her cakes was now the hub of her world. She often wondered why she had turned to cakes when eating too much had so damaged her parents. But then her cakes were works of art. They took ages to ice and were to be eaten as delicacies on special occasions. Her mother had taught her how to make the lightest of sponges and their best times together had been spent thinking up new flavours and trying them out.

It was when a speciality perfume shop had opened a few doors down, that Nicci really began to feel her dream might come true. The funny old road she had known since childhood was coming into its own. The lovely old Victorian houses were being done up and becoming sought after. A process of gentrification in the area meant that young professional people were moving in and wanting to spend their cash on luxuries. And Nicci was now determined to be the one to buy the shop.

It was touching that Nicci had such good friends as Cat who were willing to help her do up the shop. 'I honestly don't know whether I'm going to get a loan or not.'

Cat stopped in mid-mouthful and spluttered through the crumbs, 'What do you mean? Did Grant approve the loan or not?'

'He'd sort of run out of cash by the time I got there. He said he'd had more good bids than usual and it was just bad luck for me to be at the back of the queue. But he more or less said that when more money comes in, if it comes in, I might be first in the queue.'

'Oh, darn it. I guess that's just the way the cookie crumbles. But the real question is whether your loan comes in before someone puts in a good bid for the shop.'

'I know.' Nicci didn't feel like finishing her muffin and pushed it away. It had started to taste like cardboard in her mouth. 'Mr Hope more or less told me he would give me first refusal but the poor old guy can't wait forever. That shop is his retirement fund and sooner or later he's just going to have to realise the money on it.

'However kind he and Mrs Hope have been, I can't expect them to leave the shop empty too long. Empty

44

properties seem to deteriorate so quickly and that's their only asset. Still,' Nicci stirred her skinny latte absent-mindedly. 'Let's not be down, Grant Blake seemed to like my cakes.'

'Oh, he did, and so did we. He passed them around. He's very fair in that way, always tries to do his best by the staff. They were gorgeous, the best you've ever done.'

'Good. Now, what's going on with you and Luke Jones, has he asked you out yet?'

Cat screwed up her paper napkin and threw it at her plate. 'No, he hasn't and it's absolute torture for me. I'm sure he likes me; he's always looking at me and he's ever so nice at work, always offering to help me cash up if I'm pushed. Maybe he's just shy. It's just my luck that when I'm finally ready to start going out again and I've seen someone I really like he's not interested. He's very intent on his work, very focussed — perhaps too focussed to want a girlfriend.'

'Nonsense. He's single isn't he? Perhaps he just needs a push. Have you thought of asking him out?'

'Oh, I couldn't. That would look a bit desperate don't you think?'

'Not really. Lots of girls do nowadays.'

'Have you ever asked someone out?' Cat asked wryly.

'Well, no. No, I haven't. You're right. Those things sound like a good idea but they're easier said than done.'

'It might be easier if I had some sort of hobby or club I belonged to who were going out and I could see if he were interested and invite him there too. Then it wouldn't be so much like a date would it?'

'True.' Nicci wondered where Cat was going with this.

'I picked up this flyer when I was in the library. What do you think?'

Nicci looked at the leaflet. On the front was a woman in a swirly pink dress, her skirts twirling round her knees. She was dancing with a very

46

dramatic looking dark skinned man. 'What's all this about — dancing or something?' Nicci was horrified and tossed the leaflet away. She could fall over in the shower without too much difficulty. Dance wasn't her thing.

'Yup. Salsa. It's fantastic exercise, really hot and sweaty I'm told.'

'But I don't want to get hot and sweaty.'

'Aw, come on you'd try it wouldn't you? Just for me. After all, you've often said you'd like a boyfriend except you don't have time for one. Make time. Let's try it — we can go together.'

'Please Cat, I really don't think I'm cut out for that kind of thing.'

'For me.'

'I don't think . . . '

'As a thank you.'

'You're making this very difficult for me.'

'Absolutely. It'd do us both good. Then maybe once we've been a few times, I could ask Luke if he fancies tagging along and I might get my date.'

Nicci looked at Cat's wide brown eyes and dusky olive skin. She was made for salsa. She'd look fantastic twirling around in a swirly skirt flicking all that long hair at some Latin man. 'Okay. Just for you. Just once.'

'Great!' Cat bounced up, and said, 'Do you want to keep the leaflet?'

'No, no point. Just tell me when and where it is and I'll meet you there.'

'Okay,' Cat read, 'It's at the Twelve Bar Club on the High Street at seven tomorrow. Let's meet outside and we can have a quick drink to give us Dutch courage beforehand.'

'Okay, tomorrow at seven it is.' Nicci didn't know what she'd got herself into, but there was no getting out of it now.

★ ★ ★

Did she even have a skirt to go to salsa in, Nicci wondered as she walked down the street on the way back to her flat? When she got indoors, she trawled through her wardrobe. The skirt she had on now was far too business-like. There were only two others and both were dull and out of date. Jeans she had a-plenty. One pair were suitably tight and cream coloured and didn't look as if she spent her life cooking in them.

Then she looked through her t-shirts. They were all baggy and some had holes in them or dangling strings of cotton where the stitching was coming loose. She had one pretty dress but that was for warm weather and the spring chill they were getting now could in no way be called warm, especially in the evening.

But she did have the shirt she was wearing now. That would look quite cool, she decided, holding the jeans up in front of her. Almost chic, amazingly enough. With a gold necklace and bangle, she would do. Heavens, the things Cat dragged her into.

Nicci took off her smart shirt and put it in the wash for tomorrow. The suit she hung carefully on a hanger and confined to the back of her wardrobe wondering when on earth she would wear that again. Putting on familiar slouchy jeans and a comfy t-shirt and cardigan she felt much more like her old self. The only reminder of this morning's transformation was her hair, a silky, shining blonde bob smelling deliciously of the passion fruit scented conditioner the hairdresser had put on it this morning.

As so often, a single scent started to conjure up thoughts of a new flavour for her cup cake icing. Hmm, she thought, passion fruit and mango. She could do a delicate peachy coloured icing and then try and reproduce passion flowers on the top. They would do wonderfully for this week's special flavour cupcake on the stall. She had a special on every week, and people had started to come just for them, excited to know each Saturday what there was going to be to challenge their taste buds.

Nicci rifled through the magazines on a pile in the corner of the lounge. She often picked up catalogues for anything from toys to plants as research material for her tiny icing models to go on top of cakes. She flicked through, knowing what passion flowers looked like from some she had seen on sale in the market. Quickly she found a photo; they had wonderful complex centres. Fired with enthusiasm, she gathered up a scrunchie, looked regretfully at the super sleek style she was about to ruin, and jammed her hair up to keep it out of the way while she was cooking. Elegant and businesslike was great, but not when you were about to slosh about in cake mix and icing sugar.

She went to the kitchen and started to make up a batch of the special cupcakes, all the while thinking of Grant Blake and whether he was going to make her dreams come true. As she dropped a blob of dark vanilla essence into her mixture and dipped in a clean finger to taste if it were just right, Nicci considered today's meeting.

There were only two things, as far as

she could see, to stand in her way. The first was if the bank ever stopped lending money. Well, she thought as she dolloped spoonfuls of the mixture into flowery paper cases, there might be a credit crunch on but they hadn't stopped lending altogether. The only other problem would be if he found out how she had lied to him. Well, not lied to him exactly, she reasoned. More lied by omission. It was what she hadn't told him rather than what she had. But then, who pointed out their flaws to people, particularly people they wanted to impress? Who would ever say at such a meeting, 'I must tell you what a complete sham I am, listen to this you'll never believe it . . . ' No. People didn't do that.

Nicci had never told anyone her secret. She'd managed to keep it quiet and so often she wondered why people didn't find her out. Her problem always seemed to her like the silent elephant in the room. To her it was so obvious, so damaging, such a total black mark against her and yet people couldn't see it and she was so skilled at hiding it.

She opened the oven door and slid in the tray with its full paper cases. In a moment, she would look through the glass as she always did and see that wonderful transformation from gloopy mix to light puffy delectable cakes.

As she stared at the mix, watching it liquefy and become glossy, then start to bubble and finally after five minutes begin to make its slow rise up the waxed paper, she thought how devastating it would be to all her plans if Grant ever found out. He was one of the good people, the honest people who didn't lie and cheat to get through life. If he discovered what she was, the awful words people could use about her, she reasoned, he'd be sure not to grant her so much as a second glance, yet alone a shedload of money.

She watched the cakes come to that wonderful roundness, like tiny hills and breathed deep as the warm vanilla and sugar hit her nostrils. Only two minutes to go she thought as the cake mix started to turn gold, like someone tanning in the sun. Still, she reasoned, so far Grant didn't know and she wasn't about to tell him although in some ways it would be wonderful to unburden herself to someone. She'd never do that though because she would never find someone she trusted enough to help her, for help was what she desperately needed.

In a second she judged the cakes to be just right and whisked them out of the oven and on to waiting cooling racks. What was she thinking, she shook her head and practically slapped her own face to bring her to her senses. How on earth could she contemplate telling anyone, any human being about her deception, least of all Grant Blake? She gave out a little derisory laugh. Just because he had a spark of kindness about him. Yes, that was it. Although he had been cold and official, when he had told her the loan wasn't hers, he had let her down carefully and considerately.

Don't be fooled, Nicci thought as she whipped off her apron and made her way into the hallway, that's what her mother had always said. 'Never tell anyone your secret Nicci, no one, not ever. Don't be fooled into thinking it won't matter, because it will, you'll be marked out. People will despise you, they'll say you're different, stupid, less than they are. Don't be fooled.'

Her father had agreed. 'People are cruel Nicci. They'll despise you, like they despise us for not being the same as them. Just because we're different, because we keep ourselves to ourselves and because we're much bigger than they are, they'd laugh at us if we went out. Kids might throw things at us.'

'But it's difficult Dad. Sometimes I feel it would be so much better just to tell someone and get it off my chest. I nearly told Cat the other day. She's the best friend I've ever had.'

'Don't chance it.' Her father had pointed waggling his finger in the air, 'Friends are all very well, but you never know how they're going to react. And who they might tell. Once you've told one person you've told a hundred if you ask me.'

But it was difficult, thought Nicci, tears pricking at the back of her eyes. It was hellishly, horribly difficult having such a huge secret and bearing the burden on her own. Her parents had had her to help them. But who did she have? Determined not to feel sorry for herself, she grabbed her handbag. Making new flavours always cheered her up when she felt like this. It made her think of happy things. She would go off and buy some fresh passion fruit from the stall on the corner, they were good they always had exotic stuff. Ramming the front door tightly shut behind her, it was like she had slammed the door shut on her problem. Just like her parents had slammed the door of this flat tight on their problem.

No. She would never, ever, tell anyone, as long as she lived.

Suddenly she felt more positive.

When she came back, she would wash that shirt out so she was ready for tomorrow. She smiled. Salsa dancing? She'd be rubbish at it, but at least it was a night out. All of a sudden she was looking forward to the next day.

4

Cat's mother openly looked disapprovingly at Cat's skirt. 'Isn't that a bit short, darling? When we used to go dancing in my day, our skirts were below the knee.'

'Times have changed Mum.'

'What sort of dancing is it anyway?' Mrs Kincaid sniffed, looking down her nose at the leaflet. 'Salsa? What's salsa?'

'It's South American, Mum with elements of Caribbean and African.'

'Hmmph.' Cat could feel the disapproval emanating from her mother like steam from a boiling pot. 'What time will you be back home?'

'I don't know, Mum. I'm twenty-five years old. I might be back at midnight, I might be out all night for all I know.' Her mother looked aghast. Instantly Cat felt guilty. She'd never stayed out all night but Mrs Kincaid's unwillingness to cut her apron strings and stop checking up on Cat drove her crazy at times. 'Look Mum, I'm going with Nicci so we'll take care of each other. I spoke to one of the girls at work who's been and she said there's a really nice crowd and no one even drinks much because you can't drink and dance well, and that's what it's all about. It'll do me good, give me some exercise.'

'That's true dear. I only worry because I care about you. Especially after all that stuff with Mark.'

Cat felt her stomach dip at the mention of his name. It was as inevitable as day following night that her mother would bring the subject of Mark up again. Cat stood in front of the hall mirror putting the finishing touches to her makeup. 'Mum, Mark's history.'

'Such a nice young man.'

'Yes, Mum, but he belongs to someone else now.'

'Perhaps you should have tried

harder, darling. I'm sure he would have come around.'

'Mum, I wasted four years waiting for Mark to make some sort of commitment. It just wasn't going to happen.'

Mrs Kincaid wiped an errant speck of dust off the hall table. 'He really loved you, you know Catherine. I could see it in his eyes.'

Yes, thought Cat, I could see it too. It was the most wonderful feeling in the world bathing in Mark's admiration. But then it had all gone so, so bad. Mark had been a soldier Cat had met at a friend's wedding. He had approached her for the second dance and they had been inseparable the whole evening. It had been a moonlit night and the wedding reception had been at a big house with grounds running down to a lake. As midnight came, she had felt like Cinderella at the ball. He had told her how wonderful she looked in the dress she had chosen so carefully and suggested, as it was hot, that they should go and sit down by the lake.

As they listened to the hushed whisper of the water kissing the shore in the gentle breeze and looked at the moon shimmering on the water she had crossed her fingers behind her back hoping upon hope he might ask her out. When he said he desperately wanted to see her again it was the happiest day of her life.

He had been so incredibly romantic whenever he came off leave. He would buy her flowers, take her out and treat her like a princess. And each time, he came back with a charm for her bracelet. The first one was a gold 21 inside a circle to mark her 21st birthday; the second was a tiny gold horse with wings. In her letters to him, she had told him how one of the few things which made her able to bear the times they were apart was when she went down to the local stables at the weekend to help look after the horses. He had bought her a horse with wings because he said in his letter back that he dreamt some nights of flying to her side, away from the desert, the searing heat and the endless sand where he was fighting.

Those little charms had built up over the years. The last one Mark bought her was a tiny cottage. Her heart had lurched when she unwrapped it.

'One day, one day soon,' he had said curling the ends of her hair around his fingers, 'I'll buy you a cottage like that for when we get married We'll live in it together and forget about the world. We'll have our children there.' It was a promise. A promise of a future together. It was all she'd ever wanted. Since the first day she'd met him and they'd sat together bathed in moonlight. Then she'd got the letter.

She remembered that day as if it was yesterday. The pain, the excruciating tightness in her chest as she read it; crying from the pit of her stomach until she thought she could never stop; the feeling when sleep finally came, that she just wanted to sleep for ever had engulfed her like a fog. But the next morning when she woke up red-eyed his letter was still lying screwed up on her bed.

Mrs Kincaid had been beside herself making endless cups of tea. 'Maybe it's just a phase he's going through, darling. I can't believe he's really met another woman.' But he had, a nurse who had tended one of his injured friends. She understood the life of a soldier he had written. She had helped with his loneliness so far away from home. He'd wanted to break it to Cat face to face but felt it only fair to let her know as soon as possible.

Now, whenever she thought of that, Cat felt devastated.

Four long years she had waited for him. In her young eyes that felt like a lifetime. She'd put off buying her own flat, stayed living with her mother on the promise that her future was secure with him. Of all the things she had feared, that he might get injured or killed, in the end he had been stolen by another woman and there had been nothing she could do about it. It had broken her heart. The grief had been unbelievable but gradually she had pulled herself out of it and finally felt she was ready to meet someone else.

Her mother bustled about Cat, dusting and cleaning which was her standard response to any difficult discussion. In the background her mother's voice droned on, telling Cat to be careful and to watch out who she got involved with at the salsa dancing. As Cat listened with half an ear, and put on her earrings, she thought of Luke Jones.

'Can I help you with that?' was the thing she was most likely to hear from Luke. He was young and hadn't long started at the bank. Mr Blake, the Manager, had asked Cat to take Luke under her wing on his first day to help with his induction. Cat was only too happy to oblige.

She found him incredibly good looking. With spiky blonde hair and always wearing a sharp suit she liked the way he made her laugh. He charmed all the women but it was Cat who he seemed to be most interested in. So much so that the other girls giggled every time he went over to Cat to see if there was some favour he could do her.

But he'd not asked her out. She put on a last lick of lip gloss to complete her look. Her red skirt wasn't that short and besides she was wearing leggings underneath and flat shoes which she thought would be easier to dance in. If she could only learn from tonight's class a little bit about salsa, she could bring it up in conversation with Luke and invite him to next week's lesson. It might just be the push he needed.

'Goodbye then Mum. I shouldn't be late. Don't wait up for me.'

'I always wait up for you Catherine, I can't help it.'

Her mother smiled and they embraced quickly before Cat left to meet up with Nicci. She knew what her mother really wanted was to become a grandmother. And tonight, thought Cat, with a light spring in her step maybe she was just about to take the first step on that long, long road.

5

Nicci asked a passer by in the High Street to direct her to the 12 Bar Club. She hesitated at the door, hoping that maybe Cat was already there. It was dark inside with trendy blue lights flashing in the darkness. When she saw two giggling girls going in wearing low cut tops and flirty skirts she felt uneasy about whether she'd worn the right clothes. Her elegant outfit now seemed to be a terrible mistake and panic swept through her. Obviously most of the women were here to meet men.

A couple of guys who'd obviously come from work hurried past her and slid into the 12 Bar. Neither of them appealed to her; they were okay but lacklustre. She'd become so wrapped up in her business of late, men hadn't been on the agenda. But, even as a teenager she'd dreamt of escaping the restrictive life with her parents to settle down with someone special in her own home. Often in the evenings lately, the flat had seemed extraordinarily empty. She hadn't long lost her parents and their departure had left a massive gap in her life. The trouble was, when they'd been alive, they'd filled up every waking moment.

In their last years they'd become cranky and ill, both carrying so much extra weight. There always seemed to be a mountain of washing, huge amounts of food shopping and endless sinks full of washing up. Now they had gone, her spare energy had largely gone into building up her cake business. But in the quiet moments, when she woke up in the middle of the night and couldn't sleep, she had longed to have someone lying beside her, to cuddle up to and to look after her for once.

Watching the trickle of men walk into the 12 Bar, there wasn't one who sparked any interest in Nicci. Sighing, she held her head up and pushed open the door, terrified in case Cat wasn't there and she would have to hang about looking lost. Thank heavens, Cat was sitting over in a corner with two diet colas in front of her. She was studying the little group of dancers who had already gathered in the room beyond the bar and were kissing each other on the cheek in greeting. As soon as she noticed Nicci, Cat waved excitedly.

'Sit down,' she coaxed, 'It's all very interesting. I'm so pleased you're here Nicci, I couldn't possibly have gone through with it on my own. Everybody seems to know each other but look over there though, I think those guys are new like us. Isn't it exciting?'

Nicci wished she could share Cat's enthusiasm. 'I think it's just scarey. How on earth will we know what to do?'

'No idea,' giggled Cat. Let's just wait and see. Did you pay and get your hand stamped as you came through the door.'

'Yes,' Nicci looked at the green inky

splodge on the back of her hand.

'Okay, it looks like people are gathering. Let's go over.'

Nicci was glad she had a drink in her hand and found herself holding it up like a sort of shield. Then the music started playing; an infectious happy beat with bongos and a South American lilt met her ears. Two experienced dancers were trying out steps in the corner, both wiggling their hips and performing intricate turns and whirls.

'It's just like Strictly Come Dancing. You'll see, in a few weeks, we'll look just like that.'

'I doubt it,' shouted Nicci above the music.

'Okay,' came a booming voice. 'Please, if everyone has paid, come over here to find out which class you're in.'

The teacher looked South American, his sleeveless t-shirt showing off impressive biceps and cut off trousers his dancers calves. He looked more ready for the beach than a cold spring night in England. 'Good evening ladies,' he said cheerily to Cat and Nicci. 'You're new, yes? Then you need to join the beginners.' They were ushered off to one side of the bar while the more advanced dancers took their lesson on the other side.

Cat and Nicci stood in line with all the other women, facing a long line of assorted men. The teacher of the beginners' class was a woman. First she showed everyone how to put their left arm around their partner's back and hold their partners right hands up. 'Make sure you connect, there has to be sufficient tension for the ladies to be able to read the men's lead. Ladies, don't be too stiff but be aware of your partner's signals.' Then she showed them how to walk back and forwards and side to side in time with the music.

'Hey, this isn't too difficult is it?' Cat said as they completed a sequence and the line of ladies was asked to move on so that each time they got a different partner to practice with.

'I don't know that I'm quite getting

71

the hang of it, Nicci answered. I stepped on that last guy's toes three times. I don't think he's very happy.'

After an hour, they were both exhausted with concentrating and Nicci was pleased to see the lesson was over. She sat down with Cat at the side of the dance floor to sip the refreshing cold coke and watch the social dance begin. Their teacher came over to them and said, 'How did you enjoy that ladies? Not too difficult for you, I hope.'

'Oh no,' answered Cat. 'I loved it.'

'Well, you must practice now. If a guy offers you a dance it's considered rude to turn him down, and it's the only way to learn.'

That very moment, a man around Cat's age, tall and skinny but with a kind face came up and offered her his hand and motioned his head to the dance floor. 'My name's Dean, wanna try a dance?'

He'd been in their class but Nicci heard him say to Cat as they wandered off to dance that he was thinking of joining the intermediate class next.

Nicci was pleased to see Cat enjoying herself and just wished she'd been as happy in the class. Cat was doing pretty well and even managed a quick turn and was laughing and giggling with her dance partner who was giving her gentle instruction in the fine art of salsa moves.

'How did it go?' The South American man who had given the more advanced class had come over to chat.

'I'm not sure if it's really my thing,' answered Nicci. 'I couldn't quite seem to get the rhythm and I was thinking it would be better as more of a close partner dance where there wasn't so much twirling.'

'Ah', a broad smile suffused his face. 'For that you need tango. I am Argentinian. We are the best tangeuros in the world. Here,' he delved into his shirt pocket and pulled out a card. 'I teach tango too, at a Friday class at the civic hall. It starts at seven-thirty. It's mucho elegante. The ladies all wear very beautiful dresses to hug the figure and display the legs. With tango, everything is in the footwork — high heels are best.

'The civic hall is an old building and there's a wonderful big room with a wooden floor and a viewing gallery around the top. We set up a little bar in the corner and put around coloured lights to create mood. We have beginner and advanced lessons. It's very popular. People often find they are attracted either to the fast and furious nature of the salsa or to the more stately, but passionate dance of tango. You must try tango if you don't like this. A pretty girl like you shouldn't go to waste.'

From feeling miserable about not having done well in the lesson, Nicci suddenly felt uplifted by the compliment and held on tightly to the card he had given her, uttering an embarrassed, 'Thank you,' at the comment.

Perhaps he was just being a typical Latino, she thought as she watched him dance with one of the experienced girls.

They did look wonderful, and Nicci wished she could do some sort of dance. Standing bent over a kitchen top icing cakes all day made her stiff. It would be super to do something to shake out all that bending. She looked at the photograph of the dancing couple on the card he had given her. The man had sleek black hair and a sharp 30s style suit. The girl was ultra-slim and being held bent back in a passionate embrace. Her dress was chic and understated with a slight split up the side, displaying patterned stockings and graceful shoes with little diamanté buckles. They looked so poised, so sophisticated.

'Hi — what's that?' Cat was panting with effort as she came back to her seat, led by Dean.

'Oh, nothing really. It's a card advertising another dance class. The teacher said he does tango too, on Fridays.'

'I've heard about that,' said Dean. 'It's meant to be a fantastic evening.

I've thought of trying it myself some-time. Maybe,' he said looking more at Cat than Nicci, 'we could all three of us go this Friday. If you girls are free.'

'Oh, no — ,' began Nicci but her voice was drowned out by the starting up of the next number.

'We'd love to,' shouted Cat above the drums and guitars. 'You're not doing anything are you Nicci?'

'Well . . . '

'That's sorted then,' announced Dean. 'I'll see you both outside the civic hall at seven-fifteen.'

When he had gone off to get himself a drink, Cat said, 'Well, there's a result. And we're sure to lose weight doing all this dancing, not that you need to, but I could do with losing a few pounds. I'm whacked.'

'Really, Cat, I'm not sure I can come on Friday. I've got to get up early for market. I've got hundreds of cakes to make in my new flavour. I'll be really busy.'

Cat put her hand on her friend's

arm. 'Please come Nicci. It won't be the same without you. Besides, you work too much. You should play a little too.'

So that was it decided, and all Nicci could think of was that she didn't have a single, elegant fashionable dress to wear. She'd have to go out shopping again. Twice in one week she thought, and then realised that before this week, she hadn't shopped for clothes in over a year. Perhaps it was time to crawl out from inside her shell.

★   ★   ★

Grant lay in his bed thinking about the visit the police were to make to the bank the next day. It was three in the morning and he should have been asleep but instead he was wide awake. The Detective Inspector had rung him the day before and booked an appointment, telling Grant not to let on to any of the other staff that he was a policeman. Grant was just to say that he had two new employees who had been

77

sent from head office, new recruits who were here as part of their induction to learn how a small local bank operated. They were in plain clothes and keen to remain undercover.

Fraud was a serious business and thinking about what action he could take had kept Grant awake half the night. The other thing that strangely kept running through his mind was Nicci . . .

He'd only met her once, but her face kept returning to him whenever he wasn't busy. That smile was so winning, he was desperate to help her with her business, desperate — if he was honest — to see her again. A couple of times, he'd got out her file, telling himself he wanted to check on her figures but had found himself looking again and again at her phone number.

It wasn't just that she was gorgeous to look at and sparky and confident when she talked about her work. It was the contrast in her that fascinated him. There was something that Nicci was hiding about herself, he was sure of that. She did a good job of shielding herself from enquiry but dealing with people was as much part of his job as dealing with figures and he knew that there was something about that appealing woman that was guarded, something she didn't want the world to know.

He'd lain there, sleepless, for over two hours in the middle of the night, and had finally got up and gone downstairs. Pacing the lounge hadn't helped him to relax at all. As he did so, drinking hot milk in an attempt to wind down, he thought of the fraud and the faces of all his staff had passed through his mind. How could he possibly deal with whoever it was who was committing the fraud?

The Detective Inspector had seemed convinced that someone was targeting Grant's bank but had told Grant they only had a few leads. Grant's staff consisted mainly of young, fun individuals and he liked all of them. He could feel the knots beginning in his stomach as he stressed out at the thought of discovering who the culprit was, conducting a disciplinary, and eventually having them arrested.

Or, he considered, his knees giving way so that he slumped into his deep leather sofa, it could be one of the older staff. His little coterie of happily married middle aged ladies like Mrs Morton. The ones who tried to mother him. Surely it couldn't be one of those who was setting out to steal from the bank? Grant pushed the warm milk aside and watched it skin over, getting cold. Meeting the police tomorrow would be a nightmare. He must get some sleep tonight if he was to deal with this.

Idly, he picked up the remote to the TV. That was it, that would help him relax. He flicked the DVD on and brought up the programme he had recorded about Argentine Tango. He'd started classes at the civic hall about six months ago. After a good start where he'd become quite proficient, his attendance had tailed off because he'd brought home a lot of work from the bank, reading reports and things he didn't have time to do in the day.

But, he realised that was a foolish thing to do. More than ever, with the problems surrounding the fraud, he needed to try and relax. He may have resolved never to have anyone dependant upon him, never to have a wife and children because of the incident in his past which made him feel he would be such a poor provider, but that didn't have to stop him meeting people. Dance was a wonderful way of connecting with people and he seemed to be extremely popular with women, never lacking partners.

Grant enjoyed the company of women. He loved their lightness, their delicacy, the way they laughed and smiled, the pretty clothes they wore and the delectable perfumes.

He had had girlfriends in the past but had never let any get beyond a certain point. As soon as things had threatened to become serious he had backed off. He simply wasn't worthy of a woman's love, and he was terrified of anyone relying on him.

After all, years ago, he had failed the most important person in his life. Experiences like that taught you that being alone was considerably safer.

He loved the music of tango, it helped him forget. He had bought a number of tango CDs which he often listened to with a glass of wine and sometimes practiced his tango steps in his front room, pushing back the sofas. He was actually pretty good at it and the evenings he had danced tango at the civic hall had relaxed him completely, yet tired him out so he never slept badly.

As he pressed the buttons and started to watch the tango programme, he instantly felt more at ease. While he watched, he went over to the pile of papers in his filofax and pulled out the card advertising tango to remind him of the time. Then he slotted it next to his telephone where it was easy to find. Feeling easier now, he glanced at his watch. He would watch the programme for half an hour, then settle back into bed and, he was sure, get off to sleep much more easily hearing the tango tunes play in his head.

★   ★   ★

Nicci had spent days solidly baking and icing until she had boxes and boxes of different cupcakes ready for the week-end market. There were the delightful mint chocolate chip ones with a melting chocolate cake base and green minty icing. Then there were the gorgeous lemon and tangerine cupcakes with their little marzipan fruits on the top and small green leaves and finally, her piece de resistance — the passion flower and mango cupcakes. The passion flowers had worked out splendidly, their white petals with pink throats looked so exotic with the stamens she had made of sugar.

Nicci had worked hard, flopping into bed each night utterly exhausted, so she had decided to give herself Friday off to go shopping for something to wear to the tango class that night. What was it the teacher had said? A beautiful dress, something to hug the figure and high heels as you always danced tango on the balls of the feet. She had hit the shops early, wanting to get back in time for a leisurely lunch and an afternoon spent soaking in the bath so she was fresh for the evening.

As she walked down the street she had almost run out of shops to look in and was on the point of giving up. Although there were pretty dresses and brightly coloured skirts in yellow and lime green she hadn't yet seen anything elegant.

There was one shop she hadn't tried. She usually never even went in there. The prices displayed in the window were twice what she'd normally pay. But as she went past she saw they had a sale on. Shimmery fabrics, chiffon and silk nestled on the tailor's dummies as the sun streamed through the shop window. As if there were a powerful magnet at the door, Nicci felt herself drawn in, just to have a look.

There it was. On a dummy in the corner of the room. Nicci couldn't help staring, her mouth open, at the most beautiful dress she had ever seen. 'Isn't it gorgeous?' The salesgirl came and stood next to her.

'Beautiful. But I don't think it would look right on me.'

'Whyever not?' The girl lifted the cream fabric, as light as air, showing how it glimmered under the spotlights. 'This fabric is called devoré, it's superb isn't it? The overskirt is gently flared over the coffee-coloured underskirt so that when you move, it shimmers. You've got a lovely slender figure; this style would suit you perfectly. Because it's cut on the bias, it would sit close to your waist. But there's a shawl collar over the bust so it makes a small bust look more ample.' She let the material run over her fingers like water running over rocks in a stream. 'This is the last one and it looks about your size. Give me one minute to take it off the stand and you can try it on.'

Nicci had noticed the price tag and it had been reduced a number of times to bring it within her range. As the salesgirl gathered up the dress, she picked a small cream coloured silk shrug off the rail and put both items on hangers, taking them to the fitting room. 'This shrug is so perfect with the dress. It's quite demure and very simple. It tones the dress down for when you make your entrance to a room. Then, when you've been there a while and the party hots up, you can take off the shrug and really let the dress do its work. Here,' she held open the curtain to the changing room, 'While you're trying it on, I'll go and get some shoes to go with it. I've got just the perfect pair in mind.'

'Thank you.' In the quiet of the

changing room, Nicci flared the skirt out in her hands and let the light as air fabric float over her hands. She pulled down the side zip, took off her jeans and t-shirt, slipped out of her trainers and stepped into the dress. The silk felt cool against her skin, the soft fabric moulded itself to her waist and fell over her hips perfectly.

'Here,' the girl's voice behind the curtain said, 'I've found shoes in your size . . . five, isn't it? These really do set off that dress.' Her hand came around the curtain and the shoes appeared. Cream leather, they had a small strap held down with a tiny diamanté buckle. They were cute and ladylike and would be perfect for dancing, with a heel that was high enough to arch the foot but not too high to be uncomfortable. Nicci finally slipped on the shrug and opened the curtain to get a better look in the long mirror outside the changing rooms.

'Wow,' said the salesgirl. 'I'm not just saying this, but that outfit is knockout.

So feminine and pretty, and just a little bit sexy. Do you have somewhere special to go?'

'To a dance actually at the civic hall. I'm going to learn Argentine tango.'

'That would be perfect,' said the girl, smoothing down the back of the shrug. 'Are the shoes comfy?'

'Yes, they're surprisingly easy to walk in.'

'Splendid,' said the girl, obviously pleased with her skills of observation. 'I knew that dress would suit you to a T.'

As Nicci walked out with a classy bag containing the items carefully wrapped in tissue and fastened with stickers with the shop's logo, she wondered what Cat would think of her all dolled up. Ah well, it was Cat who had got her into this so she was responsible. Nicci felt special as she walked back home, swinging her secret dance clothes in the swish carrier bag. She giggled to herself to think what her regulars at the stall, who only knew her in her market garb of jeans and t-shirt, would think if they could see her tonight in her special clothes. They probably wouldn't recognise her, she mused.

★ ★ ★

'Detective Inspector Dawson,' Grant stated as soon as the plain clothes policeman and his female colleague were safely behind the closed door of his office. 'Please take a seat. Coffee?'

They both accepted. DI Dawson was a skinny, red-haired man with a pale complexion and searing blue eyes, which Grant suspected could see into the soul of any criminal.

'Thanks for seeing us today Mr Blake. May I introduce Detective Sergeant Sarah Connolly? I'm sorry I couldn't tell you everything on the phone but I'm sure you'll understand, it's better if we get to know you and your bank when carrying out this sort of investigation.'

'Indeed,' replied Grant. 'This is a very unpleasant business. I hope you're wrong and that none of my staff is operating against the bank.'

'Hmm, well we have evidence to suggest that's not the case.'

'What evidence exactly?'

'We've been conducting an under-cover operation over three counties, centring on a criminal ring. Like many such groups, they are into a number of scams to make money and launder the proceeds. One of the things they are suspected of is identity fraud. They have a forger and sophisticated equipment for producing extremely high spec documents — driving licences, passports and the like. We've been tracking some of them for a number of months but we think they may have some new recruits.'

Grant quirked an eyebrow questioningly. 'Excuse my saying, but if you already have a body of evidence against these criminals why don't you simply arrest them?'

'It's not quite as simple as that.' DI Dawson took a long draught of coffee, draining his cup. His lean frame looked the sort that existed on coffee and cigarettes. 'The sort of criminals we're dealing with are sharp, as bright as you or I. In mainstream life, it would be them who would be the senior policemen and the bank managers. But they've taken a different path and it's up to us to stop them profiting by it. It's a crying shame if we know they're up to a whole raft of crimes but we've only gathered evidence to convict them of a handful. All that does is teach them to do it better next time and get them a minimum sentence so they're back on the streets in months. They're as crafty as a truck load of monkeys. What we need is exhaustive observation, dates, incidents, witnesses. With these sort of people, you profit by playing a long game, because by doing that,' he lifted his hand, palm upwards, then formed it into a fist and brought it squarely down on the table, 'you can throw the book at them.'

Detective Sergeant Sarah Connolly

looked at her boss then added, 'We need a watertight case and evidence points to your bank being their next target. We're confident that our under-cover surveillance hasn't been clocked by them and we're sure they don't know we suspect their activities at your bank. That gives us the upper hand. We're convinced that a member of your staff is already operating for them and about to enter into a number of potentially fraudulent transactions.' Detective Sergeant Connolly obviously meant business and seemed well used to undercover work.

'Fair enough.' Grant's soft grey eyes had a touch of steel in them. His jaw was set in a determined line as he sat bolt upright in his chair, gathered a fresh sheet of paper and took out his fountain pen just in case he needed to take notes. He could feel the tension rising up through his head and nudging the back of his skull into a headache. Thank heavens he was going to do tango tonight; he knew he'd feel exhausted by the end of the day, but he'd need the relaxation and a chance to forget all this.

But for now, he must concentrate. Hard. 'Right. Let me know what you suspect and I'll do everything I can to help.'

6

The weather had changed. The afternoon sun came out of a clear cornflower blue sky and everywhere there were yellow daffodils and purple crocuses. It was the day of the spring equinox, where the length of day is equal to the length of night. Nicci had hung her new dress in the bathroom to steam out any creases. She couldn't take her eyes off it. She might not be even close to beautiful, she thought, but that dress certainly was. As she stepped out of the bath and towel dried her feet, she looked at her legs and arms; too skinny, and too pale.

Going out on a Friday like this was a new departure for Nicci. Usually after a week's heavy baking she would simply stay in with a DVD, but she was pleased she was going to be out and about among people tonight. Any sort of social activity she found scary after years of staying in looking after her parents. But, even though she had been terrified at the salsa evening and rubbish at the dancing, she had enjoyed the buzz and the music and walking back late through the dark streets.

Too often, she'd gone to bed early and lain there listening to cars in the distance, the roar of motorbikes or the sound of people laughing after a late night and felt a pang of regret at not being out there. She didn't think she could have gone without Cat. They were due to meet at the civic hall entrance and go in together.

As she lifted the dress off its hanger and draped it over her head and down over her body, she felt transformed. The material moulded to her figure, filling it out, the silken ivory tones making her skin glow. She had decided to wear her hair up and had bought a new set of tiny clips with white flowers on them. Pinning the last strand up, she was happy with the unstructured tousled style. A little mascara, a brush of blusher, a tint of olive eyeshadow to bring out the green in her eyes and she was ready.

She slipped into the little shrug, eased her feet into the comfortable shoes and covered the ensemble in her mac that belted at the waist. There, she'd do. As she grabbed her mobile phone and whizzed out of the door, she closed it on the silent, empty flat thinking that tonight, thank heaven she would not be alone.

The bus was on time and there was a bench just outside the civic hall where she could sit in the cool evening air and wait for Cat. The tango teacher was right, this dance was definitely something you dressed up for, big time. There were men in beautifully laundered white shirts and tailored trousers, some in sharp suits. And the girls all had strappy shoes on, some bare legged, some with patterned lacy tights. Skirts were variously split up the sides or wide and floaty. At least Nicci wouldn't feel overdressed. She looked at her watch. Only ten minutes to go. Where was Cat?

As she did so, she suddenly heard her phone ring. Scrabbling around in her bag, she pressed the button. 'Cat? Hi? Where are you?'

'Oh, Nicci, I'm so sorry, I won't be able to make it.'

Nicci bit her lip. 'Why not, what's happened?'

'I came home and found Zippy wasn't well.' Zippy was Cat's little Shih Tzu dog. He'd been her pet since she was in school and was part of the family. Although he was getting older now, he was still active. 'Mum said she'd look after him so I was dead set on going dancing and I've got all ready and everything. But I just can't leave him, not when he's like this?'

'Like what?'

'He's just so listless and unlike his real self, wandering around with his tail between his legs and not happy. Mum said he hasn't eaten anything today and

97

he was sick earlier. He doesn't seem ill enough to call the emergency vet but if he doesn't cheer up, I'll take him in tomorrow. He's sitting on my lap now and at last he seems settled. I'm sorry Nicci I just don't want to disturb him. Maybe if he gets some sleep he'll brighten up. You do understand don't you?'

'Yes, of course. Poor Zippy, he's such a sweetie. I don't think I've ever known him to be ill.'

'That's why I'm so worried. He's normally full of beans,' Cat said, then added, 'Guess what though?'

'What?'

'You know Dean, the guy at salsa who said he'd go to tango? When I phoned and told him I couldn't come, he offered to come round to cheer me up and bring a bottle of wine we could share. He said he's got some photos of a salsa holiday he went on with some of the people we met at the club. He's coming in half an hour. What do you think of that?'

'He seemed really friendly with everybody. That's nice of him.'

'It is. But the other thing is,' and Cat's voice was bubbling with excitement, 'I think Luke at work is on the verge of asking me out.'

'You do?'

'Mmmm. He asked me the other day if I like the group Coldplay. He said a friend of his might be getting some tickets and he was just wondering whether I liked them.'

'You do, don't you?'

'Absolutely. But more than that, I really like Luke. He's so considerate. The other day I was really struggling with this customer at work. He's a builder, he often comes in and he's always rushing off somewhere, always impatient. Yesterday the computers were playing up so I had to ask him to wait while I processed something manually. He made such a fuss, complaining really loudly to the other people in the queue. It made me all flustered and I made a mistake and had to start again. That just made it worse and he really started to have a go at me, but Luke stepped in. He went out from behind the counter and stood in front of everyone in the queue and explained what was wrong with the computer and asked everyone to be patient. I was so grateful.'

'It sounds like he really does like you and I'll bet he wouldn't have done that for anyone.'

'Who knows? Still, I told him I did like Coldplay so I'm just waiting to see if anything comes of it. It's not that I particularly want to go to the concert but I've fancied him for weeks and he's so attentive, it's just that he never makes a move.'

'I'm sure he will Cat, just give him time.'

'You will go in for the tango lesson won't you, even if I'm not there?'

'I don't know Cat, it's a bit scary.'

'Oh, go on Nicci, please, for me. If you don't go I'll feel so guilty about not turning up.'

Nicci looked at the town hall clock. The lesson would start very shortly. She was here now and all dressed up. Maybe she'd just go for the lesson, stay long enough to make a complete fool of herself and go. 'Okay, Cat. I'll try it. But I'm not promising to go next week.'

'I'm sure I'll be able to come next week. Don't judge it too soon, you may really enjoy it. You did enjoy the salsa didn't you?'

'It was fine.' Nicci was non-committal, preferring not to remember what a hash she had made of salsa with its fast and furious rhythms. Maybe it just wasn't her dance. 'Anyway Cat I really should go now or I'll miss the first part of the lesson.'

'Okay, enjoy yourself.'

'I'll try. And give Zippy a hug for me won't you?'

'Will do.'

Nicci buried her phone back in her bag and got up, taking in a deep breath. It was now or never, she just needed to get the lesson over, try not to have two left feet, then she could go home and forget about it.

* * *

Nicci's heart was pounding louder than the music as she stepped into the hall. Around the edge, there was a long low sofa where quantities of people sat, mainly changing their shoes from their outside flatties to proper dancing shoes. This looked like serious stuff. She scuttled over to one of the few spare seats, next to a middle aged lady with a very sleek French pleat in her hair and a lovely fawn coloured chiffon dress.

'Your first time?' the woman had a kind smile.

'Yes, actually.' Nicci could have hugged her for chatting. It made her feel not quite so conspicuous.

'Don't worry dear. The first few times are difficult.' She was buckling up a pair of strappy silver shoes which looked comfortably worn, as if they'd been around the dance floor a million times. 'I absolutely hated it the first few times. It was my husband who was keen on dancing, but I persevered for his sake and we became really good at it. I lost him last year, cancer it was, but I made myself continue dancing because I knew he'd want me to. I've made such good friends. It's helped to carry me through. It's terrifying at first, but you'll get the hang of it and then you'll love it.'

'Thank you for telling me that — everybody here looks as if they've been dancing for years.'

The lady folded up the neck scarf she was wearing, 'Some have, some haven't. But we all have to start somewhere.'

'This is a beautiful hall.'

'Isn't it? We're very lucky to have it and it's rarely used except for meetings and the odd wedding fair. But I love the wooden panelling on the walls and the gallery upstairs is fun if you want to look down on the dancers. Once the lesson's over, they put tea candles on all the tables and turn the lights down. It looks lovely then and they set up a little bar over there so you can have a drink. It's the best evening out and for so little money. By the way, you look absolutely gorgeous in that dress. You won't be short of partners tonight.'

Nicci didn't believe her but was grateful for her kind words. When the music stopped, and Nicci had taken off her mac, she saw that it was the teacher who was DJ-ing the music. He gave her a cheery wave and she blushed. All around her she could hear people chatting like old friends as snatches of conversation reached her ears. This was a completely different crowd from the salseros; salsa was for younger people, secretaries, students and the like.

She heard one man discussing a lady's back problem with her and he revealed he was an osteopath. Another woman chatting to her friend was talking about her job as a lawyer. Anxiety gnawed at Nicci like sharp teeth. She had read somewhere that tango with its intricate, mathematically balletic moves attracted educated people. She suddenly felt very small and very afraid. She had dressed up to be something she was not. What if any of them happened to find out her secret? There was no way she could fit in. Surely, if they discovered the thing she hid so carefully, they would ridicule her. She'd be the laughing stock.

It was no good, she would never cope. Her parents were right. She should have kept herself to herself. An overwhelming panic hit her and the only thing she wanted to do was escape. The door was an ocean away across the vast wooden hall. If she surreptitiously picked up her mac, and draped it to hide her bag, people might just think she was going to the loo. True, she had paid but what was the waste of a little money compared to the hideousness of being exposed for what she was?

'Now, my name is Leonardo. Some of you know me, some of you are new,' the teacher's booming voice filled the room as he walked to the centre of the dance floor. Nicci froze while all around her people obediently followed Leonardo and formed a circle around him. 'Let's start the lesson. Tonight we are going to do our normal walking exercises and then we are going to learn the giro, a wonderful turn where the woman walks around the man sometimes quickly, sometimes slow. It's a chance, ladies, for you all to show off those lovely skirts and pretty legs.' There was a ripple of laughter around the large circle that had gathered.

This was her time to escape. As Nicci braced herself to dash away without being noticed she turned slightly and, to her complete shock, saw the tall, straight stance of Grant Blake, the manager at Cat's bank. Nicci felt herself turn beetroot red from the top of her head to the tip of her toes. How incredibly embarrassing to be making a fool of herself in front of Grant Blake! What would he think when he saw her skulking out? And yet if she stayed, it would be worse; then he would see her making a fool of herself. She turned away, scared he would recognise her, and made a step towards the door.

'Okay people, grab a partner and let's get started.'

No one would want her as a partner. She moved to escape, gripped with panic. Suddenly a firm, unyielding grip tightened on her arm.

'You need to come to the centre of the room.' Nicci wanted to wrench free and run. 'And I don't think you can dance with a coat and bag over your arm.' Grant's voice was firm and low so no one else could hear.

'I'm sorry I was just leaving,' she hissed.

'You're making a mistake,' he whispered.

'No, I'm not. Please let me go.'

'You haven't given it a chance.' He held her with one hand and with the other, he lifted her mac off her arm placing it on the seat; then carefully peeled her bag from her grip and gently pulled her towards the dance floor.

'I . . . I can't stay, something's come up.'

'Nothing that can't wait an hour surely. Just try the lesson. You're not the sort of girl to give up on something without giving it a fair chance. Look on this as your new business venture. Listen, they sometimes bring in cakes if it's someone's birthday, and I happen to know it's Leonardo's next week. Look on it as a promotional event; bring some of your cakes and I know you'd make loads of new customers.'

Nicci's heart stopped pounding. He'd deflected her terror and made her think of the one thing which always focussed her mind. Was he playing games or was he serious? And why on earth did he care so much whether she stayed or not? Was it because he knew, but simply hadn't told her, that he was soon going to agree her loan? Her mind was a jumble of conflicting emotions, wanting to run but at the same time, seeing all these people as possible customers. Everyone was partnering up, chatting with the person opposite, saying their hellos and exchanging names. Should she stay or should she go?

Grant's grey eyes were intense. There was no smile, he seemed deadly serious. Of course he couldn't talk to her here about the loan but, she reasoned, there was every chance that was the reason he was trying so hard to make her stay. If he gave someone a loan, it figured that he'd want their business to do well. And he was right — there was a considerable potential market for her here, around seventy-five people. She'd enjoy doing tango-themed cakes, and already ideas were flooding into her head. She could decorate the cakes with sparkles and sprinkles, little models of high-heeled shoes. Gradually she felt herself yielding to Grant's hold and being led to the edge of the dance floor next to the other couples.

'Okay, now please go into practice hold,' boomed Leonardo, 'and men can you get your lady centred by performing a balanceo.'

Grant's hold was gentler on her upper arms now, but firm as he said, 'That's where the gentleman just rocks almost imperceptibly from side to side so that he can establish where the lady's weight is, either on her right or left foot. Then, if I make sure your weight is being carried on your left foot, when I take off to the right like this, you will come with me.'

Grant stepped out, as a number of the other men were doing and magically, Nicci found herself mirroring his step. 'That's very good,' he said, 'Now back again.' They moved back together perfectly and Nicci found that she was doing as well, if not better, than many of the other ladies, some of whom were a little clumsy, or tried to lead their men and were getting ticked off for it by Leonardo.

'Now,' said Leonardo as he paraded around the room, 'I want you to walk. The classic tango walk is where the feet press to the floor as you step, keep contact with the floor and transfer your weight as you walk. Ladies please wait for your man's lead and follow him exactly, concentrate on his chest for it is in the chest that the man leads the lady, forward or back.'

As Nicci found herself gently propelled by Grant's substantial chest, she found the rhythmic pace soothing. All her panic had seemed to drift away, especially now as Leonardo had put on a lilting tango track. The music folded around her so that she felt as if she and Grant were the only people in the room. Other couples floated past but she didn't see their faces, they were a blur as she felt Grant's muscular arms through the expensive material of his lightweight jacket.

'Now, keep walking, but I would like you to go into a close hold. Ladies, this way you will feel your man's lead much better. Lean slightly into him but maintain your own centre.'

Nicci felt Grant's right arm encircle

her and urge her closer to him. She couldn't remember being this close or this in tune with a man. How could it be that the cold fish who never smiled and never gave anything away, could hold her with such sensitivity? He reached out his left hand and took her right hand, enfolding it. She was suddenly acutely aware of his touch, the feel of his skin soft and warm against hers. The power of his hold governed her every move as she felt his cheek settle on hers. Wafts of fresh scented soap mixed with spicy aftershave greeted her as she breathed, her breaths coming shallowly as she nervously followed his every move. But, in his expert hold, she found she could follow perfectly.

'Good frame, Grant, perfect,' praised Leonardo as he wandered around checking on all the dancers, 'And Nicci, you are a natural, really excellent.'

Nicci felt a surge of joy rise in her stomach. Never, ever, had someone given her any praise for being good at something difficult. As she was whirled around by Grant in the circle, she saw some women who were experts but many other ladies who were struggling a little and looked unsure and ungainly. For the first time ever, Nicci had been told she was naturally excellent at something.

School had always been a nightmare for her. She had been one of the skulkers, those who lurked at the back hoping to fade away and not be pointed out. Every subject had been a struggle. The only ones she had been comfy with were cookery and maths. But here she was excelling at something. As she relaxed more, Grant who seemed to sense her every mood put in the odd double time step to fit in with the music. Amazingly, she reacted instantly and found Grant and the music carrying her along.

'Have you ever danced before?' His words were soft and close, she could feel his breath light on her ear. They were pressed so firmly together it would have been impossible to pass a sheet of tissue paper between them.

'Never,' she clung on to him. Relishing the delicious feeling as he steered her around. She felt his right arm settle subtly further up her back and without thinking relaxed further into him as he spoke. She had never imagined dancing could be like this, such a perfect sensation of being melded to someone, literally melting into their arms.

As he spoke she registered for the first time how sensuous Grant's voice was in this intimate hold, like melted chocolate. 'This is a wonderful track called Por Una Cabeza, a true tango classic. It was used in the film with Al Pacino called Scent of a Woman. That was what got me so interested in tango; the elegance, the beauty, the opportunity for a man to show off his woman, which is of course what tango is all about. And who wouldn't want to show you off in that dress. You're the prettiest woman in the room.'

Nicci gasped as the music moved up in crescendo and Grant speeded up, carrying her round and round like a tiny dancer in a music box, like a passenger on a fairground ride. It was sheer magic, the way he propelled her so tenderly and yet so expertly. She nuzzled into his neck. That seemed to be the thing to do she thought, as she glanced at the other dancers. There was no embarrassment, no holding back. Nicci had never imagined she could experience such a close and delicious experience. So this was what intimacy was — she had so often wondered.

The music drifted on and slowed down. Nicci didn't want it ever to stop. But as it slowed, Grant gradually manoeuvred her just a fraction away from him and looked down at her. 'It's quite usual for a man to look his partner in the eye for the whole dance, to lock her in his gaze, it helps them to connect,' he said, and as he did so, she allowed herself to look straight at him while they began slower steps, walking in time. His eyes held her in their misty greyness and her heart fluttered as if it were a ribbon sailing on a summer breeze. For a moment, she imagined he might kiss her, and she realised that, above all things, in this unreal, delightful, wholly romantic setting with its lilting music speeding them on, was what she wanted most in the world. The depths of her stomach surged like a massive wave crashing inside her.

Then, as the last beats of the music resounded in Nicci's ears, Grant finished perfectly, with a final flourish, dipping her in his arms, bending her practically to the floor into an elegant pose which was scary and daring all at the same time and made her cling on to him for dear life. She hung there, suspended in Grant's strong arms.

The disappointment she felt when the music ended was only matched by Leonardo saying, 'Right, now change partners.'

'Thank you so much,' said Grant as he brought her upright again and dropped his arms leaving her unsupported. He had held her so tightly, so expertly and her head was swimming with such exhilaration she felt as if she might collapse to the floor her legs felt so weak. For all his iceman exterior, for all his unsmiling slightly sad expression, Nicci found herself totally bereft when he let her go.

'You did really well, I hope you don't mind me calling you Nicci instead of Miss Tate. I'm afraid I have to find another partner now.' Grant passed her on to the next man, a skinny, brittle-feeling individual with a toothy smile, and Nicci felt her nerves return.

Nevertheless, she completed the class. She knew though that the only reason she had any confidence with the other men was because of the dance she had had with Grant. He had put her at such ease, praised her and given her confidence. He had also given her the gift of knowing what it was like to be truly in tune with a man.

At the end of the lesson she was

partnered with a man with such a substantial tummy, she had to stand on tiptoes to reach his arms. But, he was a good lead and she had listened for ten minutes to his instructions.

'That's right, now I'm going to turn you this way and you can do a forward ocho, then if I turn you back that way, you can do a backward ocho. See? It's easy once you know how.'

'Thank you. It is a bit difficult first time.'

'I'd never have guessed it was your first time. You're doing very well. But with that giro turn you know you shouldn't lean on the man. Come this way, there's a practice room off the main room, I'll show you how.'

Reluctantly, Nicci followed, wondering how Grant was doing. Out of the corner of her eye she saw him looking in her direction. But he was surrounded by three women who were laughing and joking and, as the music started up for the main evening dance, she saw one of them pull him on to the dance floor.

The next ten minutes Nicci spent in the practice room learning how to twirl. At the end, her partner took out a large hanky and wiped his glowing forehead. 'Phew, there you are m'dear, that's my informal lesson over. I'll never be another Leonardo, but I think your turns are much better now than before. I'll send you my invoice in the post,' he quipped.

'Thank you,' Nicci answered, genuinely grateful. Her confidence had increased but as she saw Grant out of the corner of her eye, dancing in the main room, she began to have doubts. He'd said lovely things to her but probably he was just being polite. She'd never be as good as some of the other women and whereas she had been on tenterhooks, concentrating and silent the whole of the lesson, they chatted and laughed easily. The feeling of elation she had enjoyed with Grant began to subside.

The rotund man was anxious to get back to the main dance now the lesson had finished. She couldn't blame him; after all, she was just an amateur. He said, 'I'm off to say hello to a few friends but you might want to go up to the balcony and have a look down on the dancers before you venture back on to the floor. I'm happy to give you a dance if you come and find me,' his eyes twinkled roguishly.

Nicci smiled and waved as she set off up the stairs. As she reached the top and came out onto the gallery, there was the lady who she had spoken to at the start of the lesson, the one who had lost her husband.

'Sit next to me,' she motioned and Nicci was glad to have the company. 'I always have a little rest up here after the lesson before I go down and have a few dances. At my age, I need to recover before I go back into the fray. But you're young, you should be down there right now grabbing all the good ones.'

'I don't think I'm good enough for that.'

'Nonsense. You were doing very well. Besides, you just need to know who to go for. Some of the men are rather sniffy and never dance with newbies. But others are really kind and only too happy to give a bit of help and to forgive you if you step on their toes. See that man there with the white shirt and brown trousers? That's Tom; he's Dutch and really nice. He always helps the beginners and is so tolerant and charming. Oh, and that lovely looking man there, dancing with the lady in the red dress.' Nicci saw she was pointing at Grant. 'That's Grant. He's a wonderful dancer, such a lovely strong lead and he never tells you off. Occasionally if you make a wrong move, he'll tell you what he's trying to do and then do it slowly so you can follow more easily. He's so good looking, so wonderful and tall I can't understand why he doesn't have a regular partner.'

As a new record struck up, Nicci watched Grant carefully steer his partner around the room.

'Grant has superb musicality,' the woman added.

'What's that?' Nicci asked

'It's basically the man's interpretation of the music. How he keeps to the beat and the tone of his moves, whether they are soft and subtle or staccato and dramatic. I think all men who have good musicality like Grant must be very sensitive, because they pick up all the nuances of the music and match them to their partner's abilities. It's a great skill and he does it superbly.'

Nicci continued to watch Grant steer the lady in the red dress around the room. She had her hand locked around the back of his neck in a close hold and danced with her eyes closed. His arm was tightly around her waist, his hand comfortably settled underneath her shoulder blade. Nicci felt a pang as she watched; she couldn't believe herself, she was actually feeling jealous of a man she barely knew and who could never possibly be interested in her except as a business proposition. Their feet moved as if they were a four-legged animal, perfectly in time with one another. What would it be like she wondered to have a boyfriend like that? Especially someone with that strong physique who could hold you protectively, enclose you in their embrace and dance you through the panic till you were safely gathered in?

As Nicci stared, she heard the music stop then saw Grant, whose ears must have been burning, look up to the balcony and see her. She quickly put a hand up to her hair, sure she must look messy, embarrassed that he should notice her skulking away in the shadows.

'Are you going down for a dance?' asked her new friend.

'Maybe.'

'Perhaps I'll see you down there then.'

But when she had left, Nicci felt very alone. The dance floor looked superb, gently lit with candles and soft lights. But how could she cope with the fact she might sit there all on her own and nobody come and ask her to dance? Quickly, she sneaked into the room trying to look as inconspicuous as possible and picked up her mac and her bag. As she reached the door, she turned to take one last look.

There was Grant again, talking to a lady over in the corner. As he spoke, he seemed to be distracted, his eyes searching for someone. Then he stopped as he saw Nicci. For the first time that evening, his look lightened, his eyes brightened and she thought he might raise an arm to beckon her over. But then the other woman who was obviously relating a very important story, gesticulated and stepped between Nicci and Grant, blocking their view of each other. In a second, Nicci crept out of the door, down the passage and away into the cool evening air.

She knew if she stayed she'd fluff things up. She didn't have the confidence to ask someone for a dance. What's more, if she tried to strike up a conversation, these educated stylish people would be sure to talk about the films they'd seen or, heaven forbid, the books they'd read and she would have absolutely nothing to say. She'd have to stand there scared to open her mouth in case they found out how stupid she was or even, if things went really badly and she started to chat with someone, they might begin to guess her secret. She'd managed to keep it hidden for so many years but how could she continue to do so, mixing with people who were so much more clever than her?

Suddenly she hated herself in her new clothes. They were a sham and so was she. Her fine dress was hidden under her plain mac and she quickly took the little clips out of her hair and buried them in her handbag. She felt like Cinderella at midnight — plain, ordinary and alone.

What's more, the local cinema had turned out five minutes before, and there was a queue twenty people long to get on the bus. As it drew up, Nicci waited patiently in line but her spirits dipped as she could see it was full and it was a good forty-five minutes before the next bus. She watched in vain as the crammed bus pulled away, when there, tall and imposing, stood Grant.

7

Grant walked slowly across the street and stood in front of Nicci. 'So you didn't like tango then?' he asked her with a slight smile.

'I liked some of it.' Like when I danced with you, like the moment you held me in your arms. 'The lesson, I liked the lesson.'

'But not enough to stay.'

'I have to be getting back.' Nicci wanted to run. She didn't know why. It was just different seeing him now in the cool night when only a while before she had drifted around the dance floor, melting in his arms, imagining what it would be like if he kissed her.

'Let me give you a lift.'

'I don't want to take you out of your way.'

'You wouldn't. Your road is on my route home.'

What could she say? Of course he knew where she lived. Her address had been on the front of her business plan. As they walked to the car, she found Grant surprisingly easy to talk to. He put her at her ease, chatting about tango and then salsa and then he told her how much he'd really enjoyed her cakes, giving her the opportunity to chat to him about something she knew. By the time they reached her road and he had parked, she found herself walking with him to her front door. 'So, this is the shop you want to buy if you get the loan — and you live above?' he asked.

'That's right.' It wasn't very late and suddenly she had an idea. 'Would you like to see the shop?'

'Very much. After all; the bank will have an interest in it if the loan does come through.'

Nicci was keeping the keys safe for her old friend Mr Hope. She opened the door to the dusty interior and, as Grant looked around, Nicci gabbled on excitedly about her plans. 'The back where the old yard is, is South facing. It's getting dark now, but if you come over here, you can just see how the sun sets. It would be ideal if I could turn the yard into a little terrace with pots and sun shades. I'm sure people would love to have coffee and cakes here, it's a real sun trap. I love living here, particularly on days when the flower market's open — the whole road comes alive. I want to paint the walls in bright colours. What do you think of cream and lavender?'

'It sounds lovely.' He smiled.

'And I know lots of the stall holders, I could fill the room with cut flowers; it would be like an old Victorian conservatory, wonderful to take tea in.'

Grant seemed to be warming to her ideas too as he said, 'These old shop fittings could look great if you polished them up and this counter display cabinet would look lovely if it were cleaned and painted and filled with cake stands and flowers.'

'Wouldn't it just?' Nicci's heart soared; he could see it all, just like she did. He wasn't seeing an old, dusty hardware shop but instead, he shared her vision of a light, bright airy paradise of tea, cakes and flowers.

'It's got real potential,' he said. 'I've just had an idea . . . I went to see a client today about a different loan, it's shorter term but it's a new funding stream and, looking at the shop now I think it would be perfect for you. What we're offering with this different loan would be more than enough to do this shop up. Here,' he pulled a piece of paper out of his jacket pocket, 'I still have the leaflet here, you could fill it in now if you wanted.'

Nicci looked aghast as he held out the piece of paper. There was an uncomfortable silence. She took it without looking at it. 'Thank you,' she said flatly.

He offered her his pen. 'It's not a long form, why don't you fill it in now? I could get the ball rolling immediately if you did.'

Nicci looked down at the leaflet in her hands. It was all just so many dots and lines and crowded print and just looking at it made her feel sick.

In a moment, Grant had picked up on her unease. He looked at her curiously. With his acute sensitivity she realised with relief that he could tell she wasn't ready. 'I'm sorry Nicci, I know lots of people don't like paperwork and it isn't fair to give you yet more to deal with after you've just battled with your business plan.' He put his pen back in his pocket. 'Just keep the leaflet, read it tonight and let me know what you think. I'll call you soon — applications need to be in by next week. If you want to apply, I'll help you.'

'Thank you.' Nicci hurriedly stuffed the leaflet away in her handbag.

'Now, why don't you finish showing me round?'

Relieved beyond measure at not having to fill in the form, she showed him the back where she would put in a brand new kitchen and the little storage area which led out to a useful loading bay. As he opened a cupboard door to get a better look, a cloud of dust flew up, sending Grant into a paroxysm of coughing.

'Oh, dear.' Nicci bustled around him. 'I'm sorry about that. The shop really is filthy. You need a drink to clear your throat. Come upstairs. My flat is tiny but I can do you a tea or coffee, or a soft drink.'

'Thank you,' Grant managed, still coughing as his throat caught on the dust. He followed Nicci upstairs where she poured him a glass of water which he drank straight off. Then she showed him to the lounge, made them a pot of coffee and presented him with one of her newest cupcakes — apple and blackberry — all laid out prettily on a tray with napkins and bone china.

'Mmm. This is fantastic.' He brushed crumbs off his smart suit. 'You really know how to present food to make it extra special.'

Nicci glowed at his praise. Before she

knew it they were talking about everything under the sun. About her childhood, her difficult time at school and about her parents and how she had looked after them. About his struggle to rise up the ranks in the bank and about his childhood in a small town by the sea, although he was clipped about that and she noticed at one point that his face become serious and dark, as if a cloud were crossing the sun. He quickly changed the subject as if he were much happier talking about her, so she chatted about the flower market and its stall holders with their larger-than-life personalities.

Tonight she had seen a totally different side of Grant. He had been so enthusiastic about her plans for the shop and such marvellous company, and the perfect gentleman, taking her back home. It was with real disappointment that she heard him say, 'Well, I really must be going, it's getting late and I don't want to outstay my welcome.'

'Of course.' Nicci got up to show him to the door. As she walked ahead of him she was conscious of her every step, conscious of having a man look at her appreciatively as he had done all evening. Her hallway was narrow and as she went to reach for the door handle she turned to hear him say, 'Nicci, I really have enjoyed this evening.'

For a moment they stood together, only inches apart and she remembered how close they had been when they had danced. Grant was superbly handsome in his smart suit and as his gorgeous grey eyes looked down on her she turned her face upwards and their eyes locked.

Slowly, tentatively, he brought his hand up to her face and lifted her chin. She had nowhere to run, but then, she didn't want to run. As his fingers touched her, her skin tingled and an electrical charge shot through her. Like a flower turning to the sun, she nestled into the palm of his hand as he held it softly against her cheek. Then, as if they were drifting in slow motion he brought his lips lightly down on hers and pressed them for a moment in a kiss that robbed her of her breath. The moment seemed to last forever as she felt the warmth of his lips invade hers and the pit of her stomach flipped like she was dropping down, down in a speeding lift.

Nicci could feel herself floating in his embrace as Grant gently cradled her waist in his arm and pressed her to him. Tentatively, surprising herself, Nicci brought her hand to the back of his collar to feel the softness of the curls at the nape of his neck as she eagerly returned his caress. For those delightful lingering seconds, only the two of them existed.

Nicci felt herself drifting away becoming light headed, feeling Grant's warm, firm chest pressing urgently against her. Time seemed to stand still, the clouds halted in the night sky, the rest of the world slept, while these two people entwined and nothing else mattered but those endless minutes.

When he released her, she felt bereft, she could feel herself crashing back down to earth, back to reality with a bump as she suddenly became acutely conscious of the rapid beating of her own heart in her chest.

'Thank you for a truly wonderful evening,' he said and within moments he was gone and her little flat had never felt so silent and empty.

★   ★   ★

Detective Sergeant Sarah Connolly and Detective Inspector Dawson were playing their parts fantastically well, pretending to be graduate recruits sent from head office to learn how a local bank worked and carry out a study of staffing levels. 'That way, we can go undercover with your employees, mingle in and become friends and wait until one of your employees drops their guard,' they had told Grant in his office on their first day at the bank.

'Are you going to tell me who you suspect?' Asked Grant.

'Well, Mr Blake,' replied DI Dawson, 'it's better for you if you don't know initially, in case you start to treat people differently. All we can tell you is that we have two prime suspects. But we think only one is the guilty party. As soon as we start to move in, we'll tell you who it is, that's when we'll need your help to capture him, or her.'

The plan was that DI David Dawson and DS Sarah Connolly would shadow each member of staff for a period of time pretending to learn how each of them did their jobs. On the first day, DS Sarah Connolly was introduced to Cat and DI David Dawson was introduced to Luke Jones, initially over a cup of coffee in the staff room.

'So,' said Luke. 'What do you need to know?'

'We're doing a report back to headquarters about staffing. There's a fear that staffing levels are too low and we're just finding out who does what and feeding that back for the bank's five year plan.'

'Phew,' said Cat when she and Luke were alone later in the day, and packing up their things after DI Dawson and DS Connolly had left. 'That Sarah and David seem to want to know everything about what we do. I was exhausted just answering their questions and they do make a terrific amount of notes, don't they? But I suppose it's a good thing if they think we might need more staff — at least they're not thinking of making staff cuts.'

'Yes,' said Luke. 'I know I want to keep my job. I'm thinking of getting a small flat soon with a mortgage and everything.'

'Are you?' Cat found that the more she knew about Luke, the more she liked him. He was making his way in the world and settling down just as she'd hoped to do. She thought of the little charm Mark had bought her of the cottage; it now languished discarded at the back of her jewellery drawer. That was all a pipe dream after Mark's infidelity came to light. But setting up in a flat with someone would suit her just fine and Luke was always so helpful and he was funny too and she loved men with a sense of humour.

'That's my aim,' he replied, 'a flat in Filmington would be nice. I like the market there and it's an up and coming area. By the way, Cat, do you remember I asked you if you like Coldplay?'

'I do.' Cat gasped. This was it — Luke was going to ask her out!

'Well, I've managed to get tickets for a concert in London next month, on the twelfth. Would you like to come?'

'Yes,' Cat breathed again. She thought he was never going to ask. But next month was such a long time away, she wished it was sooner, or that Luke had asked her to go for a drink or something. But he could be shy and it would be something to look forward to. 'I'd love to come.'

'Well,' Luke sounded relieved, as if he'd thought she might say no, 'great, that's great.' There was a silence and Cat felt even more attracted towards him because of his shyness. Then, as if he wanted to get back onto a work footing so he would be less embarrassed, he said, 'Tomorrow, why don't I help you with some of your new accounts? I could give you a hand with the paperwork. I'm not desperately busy at the moment and we're not being shadowed tomorrow by David and Sarah, they're moving on to work with Mrs Morton and Mrs Egerton, so we won't have them to worry about.'

Cat looked at Luke and felt butterflies whirl in her stomach. There was nothing she'd like more than to have Luke work closely with her. She was snowed under at present and, as always, he was happy to come to her aid. 'That would be great. Thanks Luke.'

As she went home that night, she wondered what sort of small gift she might be able to buy Luke to say thank you for his help and for the Coldplay ticket. She didn't want to be too forward; it was always best to take things carefully especially if you've had a bad relationship beforehand — and nothing could have been worse than her experience with Mark. Maybe she'd get Luke some chocolates, that would be about right; nothing too personal, just a simple thank you from one workmate to another. That shouldn't scare him off or embarrass him.

As she headed for the Belgian chocolate shop, her mobile bleeped with a text message. It was Dean, the salsa dancer she had met the other night, texting to ask how Zippy was and if she was going to salsa again this week.

Well, thought Cat. It never rained but it poured. Not only did she have Luke Jones asking her out to concerts, but she had Dean asking her to salsa. Men were like buses — one minute there were none and the next they were coming along in twos. She'd enjoyed the salsa and Dean had been really sweet about Zippy. She texted him back to say that Zippy was okay and yes, she would be going to salsa — and then made off towards the chocolate shop with a new lightness in her step.

Life could sometimes be very exciting and full of possibilities.

8

Grant couldn't get Nicci out of his head. She had looked so utterly, totally, fairy tale gorgeous the other night. When she had sunk into his arms, he had never experienced such harmony, such resonance with another human being. She was delicate like a china doll, graceful like a ballerina. She had been streets ahead of any other woman that evening and from the moment he saw her, he had known he wanted to kiss her. When he had finally plucked up the courage and she kissed him back, she had made him feel complete as if they could be two halves of a whole, if only . . .

But something had bothered her. When he had shown her the leaflet about the other loan, she had gone as white as snow. It had seemed to frighten her and he wanted to know why. Did she have bad debts she had kept from him? So many people did.

One thing was certain, he couldn't get Nicci out of his mind. Grant paced up and down his office in the bank. He simply wasn't functioning, spending all his time dreaming about Nicci. The only cure for it would be to make contact with her. He desperately wanted to see her again.

Suddenly there was a knock at the door. DS Connolly and DI Dawson entered, interrupting Grant's train of thought. 'What can I do for you?' he asked motioning them to a seat.

'We've interviewed nearly half your staff now, and we have a few questions we wanted to ask you about one woman in particular.'

'Oh yes.'

'Mrs Morton — how long has she worked here?'

'Just under a year.'

'Did you know she had serious financial and personal problems?'

'No, she's never discussed anything with me.'

'We've been doing some background work and have discovered that her live-in partner has been in jail for fraud.' DI Dawson let his words hang on the air, letting the implication of them sink in.

'That doesn't necessarily mean that Mrs Morton is involved in anything. She's a good employee, reliable and solid. Surely it's not good to judge someone by the company they keep.'

'Your loyalty to your employee is admirable Mr Blake. But we think it's worth further investigation. It's particularly interesting that she's kept her partner's background a secret from you. You'd think she might have told you in confidence, just so that you knew.'

Grant pondered DI Dawson's words. 'It's true that employees who are totally honest and upfront will often tell me things in confidence so that I hear it from them before I hear any rumours.

They know I wouldn't break a confidence, but then I have had no reason to doubt Mrs Morton's work up until now. Above all, I think we should keep an open mind.'

DS Connolly and DI Dawson got up to leave. DI Dawson narrowed his eyes and his expression was sour. 'Forgive us, Mr Blake, but when you spend a lot of time with criminals, delving into the seedier side of life, you can find it difficult to give people the benefit of the doubt. We have to cover every avenue. We'll keep you posted.'

As he let them out, Grant closed the door with a sigh. This atmosphere of suspicion was weighing heavily upon him. He liked Mrs Morton, she was dedicated, often stayed late and never made a mistake. Now he began suspecting her too and it made him feel uncomfortable. He wished he had someone at home with whom to share such concerns and his mind flitted back to the vision of Nicci in her creamy dress, looking like an angel.

He had vowed to himself not to get seriously interested in a woman. Who was he to think he could be any woman's knight in shining armour, the sort of protector every woman wants in a partner? He was rubbish at protecting anyone. A flashback came into his mind of a sunny day many years ago. Of a beach, of happy children playing by the sea.

Then with horror he saw in his mind's eye an upturned dinghy, a hand reaching out for help and disappearing forever beneath the deep blue waves. Why did other memories fade and yet that one stayed with him as clear as if it was yesterday? He must find something positive to distract him.

Nicci Tate was a distraction. Her problems intrigued him as much as her simple beauty beguiled him. Why hadn't she leapt at his offer to apply for the other loan? She was hiding something from the world and he knew as well as anyone how stressful that was. He picked up the phone to ring her then plonked it back despondently. They hadn't agreed to meet again; he hadn't wanted to ask her, hadn't wanted to frighten her by moving too quickly. It was Saturday today, half-day closing at the bank, and the thought of a weekend on his own loomed like a deep empty chasm. Normally he was happy with his own company, but the need to see Nicci again was too hard to bear.

Then an idea struck him like a thunderbolt. Of course! It was the weekend and she ran her cake stall at the market in Filmington on Sunday. He could go and see her there. He didn't want to get in the way, so he'd go towards the end and see if he could give her a hand clearing up. It must be hard for a woman running a stall like that all on her own.

He could say he had just come to see how business was, and then he'd take it from there. Maybe if she was free she might agree to come to dinner with him.

Instantly he felt revived. Things were looking up. He found his head filling with thoughts of Nicci so much that he almost forgot the problem of the fraudster and the shadow of his own past.

*　　*　　*

Cat didn't think she could have enjoyed a morning's work at the bank better, even though it was a Saturday. Everyone seemed to be happy, even the normally cool Grant had come out to chat with them. But the best thing was that Luke had helped her all morning.

'You must like paperwork,' she joked with him as he filled out another of her forms. She had work to do on her till and the best thing was how close he seemed to want to sit with her. A couple of times, as they had been chatting, his arm had even brushed hers sending the most delicious shiver across her skin.

'I don't mind paperwork at all,' he

said. 'I wouldn't have joined a bank if I did, it's just something you have to put up with isn't it? I'm happy to help, any time, especially for you.'

He glanced at her then looked away shyly. Confident one minute, shy the next, that was Luke. Cat found it endearing.

Later that day, she was chatting on the phone to Nicci. 'Dean's so different from Luke. I find Luke complicated but fascinating, I never quite know where I am with him. One minute I think he'll ask me out, the next I don't know. Still, we've got the Coldplay concert booked so that might be the start of something. Meanwhile, Dean's lovely to go to dancing with. He's got a good job as a carpenter and he actually carved me a beautiful box in wood. It must have taken him ages. He said it was to cheer me up because Zippy's under the weather again.'

'Oh, Cat, I'm so sorry,' Nicci sympathised.

'Dean's been wonderful. He drove

me to the emergency vet first thing this morning before work and waited for ages and ages while they did some tests on Zippy, then gave me a lift to work. He's coming over this afternoon and we're going out for a meal tonight. He said he wanted to cheer me up.'

'Dean seems very keen, maybe he's a better bet than Luke.'

'But Luke is so good looking and funny. I'm pretty sure he's going to move it to a much more personal level soon but he's very busy. He still lives at home with his mum like I do. But she's ill and he spends a lot of time helping her. That's sweet, don't you think?'

Nicci did think it was nice, but thought that if Luke were really interested, he could have invited Cat over for a meal or coffee at his house, even if he had caring responsibilities. Whereas Dean seemed keen enough on Cat to drop everything for her.

Nicci wanted the best for Cat especially after she had had such rotten luck with Mark.

'I must go now Cat, I have a heap of things to get ready for market tomorrow. Take care, and keep me posted on how Zippy's doing.'

'Will do.'

★ ★ ★

Sunday morning dawned bright, sunny and warm. The market was thronging with crowds and Nicci sold boxes and boxes of cupcakes, the pocket in her zipped apron bulging with the takings. If only she had a shop, she knew she could have sold even more. But she was delighted with all the compliments her passion flower cupcakes had received.

Her feet were aching as she stacked the large empty trays ready to load them into the yard behind the shop. Mr Hope had said she could store stuff in the shop even though she hadn't been able to buy it yet. She was beginning the difficult task of unwinding the cover over her market stall when she heard a voice behind her say, 'Here, let me give you a hand.'

Her heart missed a beat as Grant Blake waded in and rolled the canvas cover down as if it were a paper hankie. Normally it took her ages to deal with the heavy canvas. She would hardly have recognised Grant in his weekend casuals. Faded jeans clung to muscular thighs and a clean white t-shirt showed the perfectly sculpted biceps she had felt through his jacket when they had danced.

The memory of his commanding hold and of his kiss made her blush and stutter. When he hadn't phoned she had thought he wasn't interested in her. Perhaps he was just more shy than his serious exterior let on.

'Thank you.' How on earth could she remain casual when she had spent the whole of the night before thinking about him? Her cheeks were burning pink as she remembered how this incredibly good looking, coolly elegant man really had taken her in his arms and passionately kissed her. He wouldn't want to now he had seen her in her working clothes, she was sure of that. Self consciously she tucked an errant lock of hair behind her ears.

He bent down and picked up five crates in one go. 'Where do you want these?' he asked.

'It's so kind of you to help. If you really don't mind everything can go in the back of the shop. Mr Hope allows me to keep supplies there even though I haven't been able to buy the shop yet. He's always done everything he can to help me and he said I might as well use the place rather than have it sit there empty being of use to no one.' It was ideal that her market pitch was just outside the shop.

'Did you have a good day's business?' asked Grant who had carried everything in for her in the fraction of the time it took her on her own.

'Yes, very. I could have sold more if . . . '

'If you had a shop.' Grant gave her a wry glance.

'I'm so sorry, that wasn't meant as a criticism of the bank or anything.'

He held up his hand. 'No worries, I didn't take it as such. I can see your cakes have gone, well, literally like hot cakes!' He laughed.

Nicci liked the sound, thinking he should let himself laugh more often. Once they had put all the crates away and Grant had helped her pull the covers down and locked up the stall he turned to her. 'I'm sorry to have come unannounced. It's just that I had a free evening and I was wondering if you'd like dinner. I guess I should have rung but, well, I picked up the phone at least ten times and then put it down again. Sometimes it's easier to see someone face to face. I quite understand if it's not convenient.' He went to turn away.

Nicci, who had not been looking forward to an evening alone, felt cheered by his invitation, all the more so for its unexpectedness. The tiredness

155

of the day faded from her. 'That would be lovely. Could you give me a few minutes to change?'

'Certainly, I'd quite like to check out the shop in the market that sells junk and antiques, I can kill some time there. Will forty-five minutes be enough?'

It only took forty minutes for Nicci to shower, wash and dry her hair and change into the white jeans and shirt she had worn to the salsa class.

'You look lovely,' he said. 'We could try the French bistro on the corner if that sounds okay with you,' and as they strolled off down the market road, Grant's hand stole into Nicci's, causing her heart to thrill.

This road where she had strolled a million times, which had seemed so ordinary, so mundane, now felt so different. In Grant's company the colours were more vivid, the little Victorian houses more cosy, the early evening air warmer than ever.

'What will you have to eat?' asked Grant handing her the menu.

She put it straight down. 'I'm too tired to decide. I'll have what you're having,' urged Nicci.

Over a glass of chilled Sauvignon Blanc and paté followed by grilled salmon, they talked and talked about everything under the sun. As the coffee turned up, with mint chocolates to accompany it, Nicci said, 'I wish you'd tell me something about growing up by the seaside. It sounds wonderful.'

When she saw that old familiar cloud pass over his features again, she thought he would brush her off and change the subject.

But instead, this time, he leaned forward and touched her hand, so tenderly and said, 'There's something I need to tell you Nicci. Something about my past. I've never let a woman get close to me because of my past and when I tell you, you'll probably back off too. But I can feel that there could be something special between us and I couldn't bear for that to start growing and for hopes to be raised and then dashed.

'Years ago, I did something — or rather I didn't do something — which I should have. Something that happened when I was a child that has stayed with me forever and simply won't seem to ever let me go,' he said sadly.

'We can't necessarily be responsible for things we do as children,' Nicci reassured him.

'You say that, but I've always felt responsible, I've always blamed myself and felt that my failure means I couldn't ever have someone . . . a woman . . . rely on me and look up to me. I'm just not worth it. I don't want to spoil this wonderful evening by focussing on sad things, but at the same time, I think you ought to know. I know you probably won't want to see me again and I wouldn't blame you for that.'

Nicci shook her head, but he gripped her hand tightly and went on. 'But I know I'm beginning to have feelings, real feelings for you and besides, holding on to my past has stopped me . . . with any woman and, well, you're different and I need you to know, even if it does make you walk away.'

Nicci wanted to speak but she was scared of making Grant stop. He had to go on for both their sakes. She saw him gulp, saw the lines gather on his forehead. 'When I was young,' he started, 'I had an older brother; not much older, I was twelve and he was fifteen. He was everything I wanted to be; strong, funny, daredevil, everyone loved him. I was the quiet one, studious and safe. Rafe was the one everyone looked at, the one everyone's eyes turned to. He was top in the sports teams and in academic subjects. Rafe was so vital, so full of life. We lived in Cornwall and he used to play on the beach all the time. He was teaching me how to surf. He loved to teach me things, loved having a little brother.

'One day the weather was so beautiful, he said, 'Let's take a rowing boat out and go fishing'. My father had warned us about the currents and forbidden us to go out on our own, but Rafe was sure he could handle things . . . and he did for a while. We went out, beyond the rocks, out into the open sea, larking about, casting our lines for fish.

'Then, the weather started to change. The sunny skies grew grey, then black. I told him we should go back but he said it would clear. Instead, the sea started to swell. I remember it as if it was yesterday, I relive every second over and over. He was still standing in the boat as the waves lurched. I grabbed the oars and started trying to row back to the shore, but it was impossible, the oars kept clipping the waves. I was concentrating on the water when suddenly there was this awful cry. Rafe had slipped and gone in. I held out an oar to him and screamed at him to grab it, he kept swimming as hard as he could towards me, trying to grab the oar but the swell kept pulling him down.

'Then, a huge wave rode up and threw him against the side of the boat. I could see he was stunned and momentarily he lost his ability to fight. I stood in the boat, clinging on, knowing at that point I should have jumped in to save him. He revived, grabbed for the oar but missed it. It was then I realised it was too late. He sank down, bobbed up again with his arm held high out of the water, then . . . then that was the last I saw of him.' As Grant told the story, he looked older, careworn and that sadness that sometimes threatened to engulf him was more apparent than ever.

'I waited for ages, for what seemed like hours, I rowed round and round looking for him but nothing. When the coastguard finally came, they looked too but he was gone. His body was washed up three days later.

'I should have jumped in, I should have saved him, for heaven's sake — I was his brother.'

'No,' said Nicci, at first quietly, then

again, louder. She dropped her voice as a couple next to them glanced over. 'No, no you shouldn't. Don't you see that if you had jumped in, you wouldn't be here today either?'

'You're just trying to make me feel better, but I can't change the past.'

'No I'm not,' she cried, 'I'm just trying to make you see sense. No one could have expected you to save Rafe. You were only young. Would it have been better if your mother had had to bury two sons? Those waters off Cornwall have horrendous currents, you wouldn't have stood a chance. You would never have been able to save him. Don't you see? If you hadn't had the sense to look after yourself, your poor parents would have suffered a double tragedy. At least they still have you.'

Nicci watched Grant look up at her. She searched deep within him, 'Believe me, you did the right thing. That was a horrendous decision for someone so young, but you did do the right thing.'

A thousand emotions crossed his face until, with hope in his eyes he finally spoke. 'I've never talked about this to anyone. My parents are very old fashioned, very stiff and formal. We've never discussed Rafe. It's as if talking about it relives it all again. But with you Nicci, I just felt I could; you're a strong, intelligent woman. I've never wanted to share that moment with anyone before. And all I've ever felt is blame, mostly because my parents avoided talking about it, as if they were ashamed of me.'

The waiter brought their bill and, as they wandered hand-in-hand back down the street, they talked some more until Nicci felt that she really was getting through to Grant. Before they reached her flat, there was a small green with a bench and they naturally sank into it, so engrossed were they in conversation. Finally, Nicci couldn't stifle a yawn.

'Heavens,' said Grant 'it's late and you've had a hard day Nicci.' He pulled her to her feet. 'I'm so grateful to you for all you've done. Something about this evening has . . . opened a door for me. It's like I can see light where before there's only been darkness.'

'It was nothing.'

'It was everything.' As he said this, Grant enfolded Nicci in his arms. He was warm and strong and she turned her face up, yearning for his kiss. When it came, it was hotter and deeper and more passionate than their first kiss. She felt cosseted, adored and so, so special. Her skin tingled from the tips of her toes to the top of her head and all her senses were teased as she tasted his lips of coffee and mint. She ran her hands over the soft cotton of his t-shirt and she could feel the deep breaths of passion filling his chest as he held her tight, so tight, their kiss long and hard and lingering.

As he took his lips from hers, his voice was husky, 'I want to pick you up and carry you away with me, Nicci.'

She threw her head back and

laughed, the cooling air contrasting with the warmth of their embrace. This evening was the best, the absolute best!

When he released her he said, 'I almost forgot, I've got one thing more for you.' So saying, he took out of his pocket a package wrapped in brown paper. 'I bought it from the little antique shop earlier, just because I thought you'd like it.'

Nicci untied the string as Grant watched eagerly. Perhaps it was a box for keeping her icing tools in, but it was too heavy for that. When she tore off the paper and saw what was inside, she was so horrified she nearly threw the present away as if it had been a red hot brick. 'Oh,' she gasped. A book, the worst present anyone could ever give her.

Grant was oblivious as he stood over her shoulder, opened the first page and pointed out some wording, 'It's a little cookery book just about cakes, see — it's even signed, by the great chef himself, Escoffier. And he's put in a lovely message about great cooks. And you are one Nicci. Read the message . . . go on read it.' But then he looked down at her expression and suddenly his smiled turned to a frown. 'What's wrong? What have I done?'

'I can't.' Her words were flat and lifeless. She stared at the lettering. It was all dots and lines to her; it meant nothing.

'Can't what? I'm sorry Nicci, I've offended you in some way, but I don't know how.' Grant looked horrified.

Nicci opened her mouth, but no words came out. She stood in silence gawping like a goldfish. Her whole world had crashed around her and all she wanted was for the ground to open and swallow her up.

'Oh, heavens,' realisation suddenly dawned on Grant. 'You . . . you can't . . . you can't read.' He grabbed her by the shoulders. 'Why couldn't you tell me? It all makes sense now. That's why you wouldn't fill the other loan form in. That's why I saw books on your shelves that were upside down . . . now it all makes perfect sense. You can't — '

'Can't read. No,' Nicci spat out the words. 'No, I can't read. Go on, laugh at me.' Anger boiled in her blood — at her parents so wrapped up in themselves, at her complacent school, at the rest of the world that took reading for granted. But most of all her anger was directed at Grant for finding her out.

All the frustration of years welled up and exploded like a volcano. 'I'm illiterate, stupid and uneducated. I missed school, I slipped through the net. I'm a sham, a liar and a cheat. I've had to connive and weave and bob through life at every turn to hide it. So you can take your rotten book,' she snatched the book and threw it into the bushes, 'because I won't need it.' With that, she turned tail and ran like a terrified animal.

Nicci could hear Grant shouting at her, running behind her telling her to come back, but she couldn't. Her ears filled with a roaring rushing sound and she fled to the door of her flat, jammed the key in the lock, slammed the door behind her and sped upstairs.

She wouldn't answer Grant's bangs or ringing at the door, nor her phone which rang again and again. Grant had discovered her hideous secret, that she was an illiterate idiot. How could she have been so stupid as to let anyone get that close? Especially someone as handsome — as dangerous to her equilibrium, she now realised — as Grant. She'd let her defenses slip. He'd never approve a loan now, the shop was an empty pipe dream.

As she threw herself across the bed and sobbed bitter wracking tears, she resolved never, ever, ever to speak to him again.

9

Grant had been awake all night. First he paced up and down the living room, then he tried to ring Nicci again, even though it was the middle of the night. At one point he sat down to write her a letter at which he threw both the screwed up piece of paper and the pen at the wall realising what an idiotic notion that was!

He got to work before dawn — what else was there to do? He would go mad if he didn't stop thinking about Nicci, although there must be some way to get through to her. The first thing Grant did when he got in the office was to look up illiteracy on the web. There were loads of useful sites and the more he discovered, the more he began to fashion a plan. He was a quick reader and he read voraciously, printing off as many details as he could find about illiteracy, filing them away neatly in a ring binder.

It was while he was deeply engrossed, that a knock came at the door. DI Dawson and DS Sarah Connolly stood waiting to be let in.

'Come in, come in.' Grant tried not to sound impatient but, for him, the importance of the fraud had taken a back seat. Nicci seemed to be the only thing that really mattered to him now.

'Sorry to disturb you.' DI Dawson motioned to his assistant to sit down and then he began. 'We've found out who is the mole in your bank, which of your staff members is planning to rob you and then take off.'

'Thank goodness for that,' Grant tore himself away from thinking about Nicci and, as he sat down in his large leather chair, focused on what DI Dawson was saying. 'Are you absolutely certain? Can you tell me who?'

'We're very sure Mr Blake. It's Luke Jones.'

'Luke? But he's our rising star, are you sure?'

'Absolutely.'

'Then Mrs Morton had nothing to do with any of this. You suspected her for a while didn't you?'

'We did, but she's as clean as a whistle, despite having a dodgy husband. Just because he was involved in fraud doesn't mean to say she is. She's clean. No, it's Luke Jones who's our man. What's more, he was planning to pin the blame on one of your other staff. Our techie guys have been monitoring the computers and it's a clever scam. It seems our friend Luke Jones was planning to land Cat Kincaid with the blame.'

'Cat. Oh, no, poor girl. I overheard her saying the other day that she and Luke were on the verge of going out. She's crazy about him.'

'I'm not surprised,' said DS Sarah Connolly. 'He's been all over her like a rash, playing the part of Mr Helpful, offering to give her a hand with her documentation, jumping on to her terminal whenever he gets the chance to 'help her out'.'

'In reality,' explained DI Dawson, 'what our Luke was doing whenever Cat was momentarily occupied elsewhere, was to open a number of bogus accounts while logged on at Cat's computer terminal with her code number. We discovered what he was up to by studying CCTV footage and timing exactly the moments he was pretending to help her, but in truth was logging on as Cat Kincaid. The plan was that he was going to pick his moment and then transfer sizeable sums of money from a quantity of large corporate accounts — not too much to raise immediate suspicion, you understand, but enough to make him and his cronies rich. Then, as soon as they were ready to fly, they'd draw out the monies. Once they'd done that we wouldn't have seen them for dust, they'd be off and away, abroad most likely, until they were ready to come back with different identities to carry out the same sting again. And Cat Kincaid would have got the blame.'

'That's a really hideous thing to do.'

'With your help Mr Blake, we want to pull Cat aside when she comes in this morning. She always arrives before Luke. If you keep her safely out of the way in this office with you, that leaves us free to move in on Luke the second he arrives. I'm looking forward to seeing the look on that kid's face when we let him know we've got him sussed. I've got some uniformed officers waiting in case he tries to do a runner. Meanwhile, some other uniforms will be over at his place, arresting the others in the gang.'

'But I thought Luke lived with his housebound mother.'

'Don't make me laugh,' sneered DI Dawson, 'That was just another of Luke-butter-wouldn't-melt-Jones's stories. Nothing about that kid is straight. He's a walking inventory of lies.'

When Cat arrived, Grant played his

part perfectly. 'Ah, Miss Kincaid, he called to her as soon as she'd got her coat off. 'Could you spare a moment please, in my office?'

They were able to see Luke being arrested through the glass partition and it was all a terrible shock to Cat. Grant spent the next hour giving her coffee and lending her hankies to mop up her tears. At the end of it, Grant said, 'Do you feel a bit better now, Cat?'

'I do, thanks to you. You've been very kind to me Mr Blake. I suppose I've been rather gullible.'

'Don't beat yourself up over it, Cat, we were all taken in by Luke. As long as you're feeling okay now. I don't see there's any way you could go back to work today though . . . let me take you back home so you can rest . . . Or . . . ' he said hopefully, 'I could take you to your friend's, Nicci Tate?'

'Would you, Mr Blake?'

'Grant, please call me Grant.'

'Okay, Grant. Actually I would rather see Nicci before I face Mum, that's for sure.' Then Cat said, 'I didn't know you knew Nicci and I were friends.'

'Yes, she told me. In fact, Nicci and I have been seeing each other and there's a way you can help her out if you want.'

'Of course I'll help her out,' said Cat, puzzlement and concern etched in her face, 'She's like a sister to me. Is Nicci in some sort of trouble?'

'No, no, not at all.' Grant smiled, not in the least surprised that Nicci inspired such loyalty. 'Let me get you another coffee and I'll explain . . . '

* * *

It was three coffees later before Cat and Grant set off together to go and carry out the plan that Grant had formed, and which he hoped above hope might bring Nicci back to him again. As he opened the car door for Cat, Grant had a moment's hesitation. This might work and yet it might not. Would Nicci hate him for using her friend in this way? He had had to tell Cat the whole story and in doing so, betray Nicci's secret. Would Nicci ever forgive him?

Sometimes, he resolved, you had to take risks in life.

Grant shut the car door decisively, settled in the driving seat and fired up the engine. As he sped through the streets towards Nicci's flat, his mind was racing. He'd missed one chance in his life to make a difference, years ago. But he wasn't much more than a child then. Now he was a man and Nicci was the one person who had been able to get through to him. She'd given him the key to forgive himself. Even if she didn't want him, he was going to help her. After all, darn it, he was falling for her that much was certain.

It was now or never, he knew this was his one chance to win her back.

Grant parked around the corner from Nicci's flat. When he'd explained everything to Cat, and taken the huge risk of telling Cat about Nicci's secret, she'd gasped in amazement. 'She can't read? Oh, my goodness, that explains so many little things. The way Nicci always asks people to read things for her — she says she's rubbish without her glasses and yet she never remembers them.

'It also explains the computer stuff, I've seen her do her accounts on the computer, she's fine with numbers — actually she's a whizz with spreadsheets — but she always does the columns in colours to differentiate them rather than doing headings in words. She always told me she just finds it easier that way . . . you know, red for expenditure, green for income. I thought it was quirky of her but then she is quirky in so many ways, that's what makes her fun. But then she said she can't manage word processing programmes. I always thought it was the IT she had problems with, I never guessed it was the words that were the problem.'

'So,' Grant urged Cat. 'You'll ring on Nicci's door, tell her all the stuff about Luke and then give me a ring? I feel really bad about tricking her like this, about using you to get her to open her door, but she won't speak to me. Please help me, Cat. I'd like just one more try with Nicci. She . . . well, she's beginning to mean a lot to me.'

'Don't worry, Grant. I've known Nicci for years, she can be proud, but sometimes, you have to be brave and push your friends to accept help. I'll ring you, as soon as I've done telling her about Luke.'

10

When Nicci saw that it was Cat at the door and not Grant she felt relieved, but perversely, disappointed at the same time. There was no way she wanted to see Grant, after all, she'd spent all evening and even once during the night, resolutely refusing to answer his calls and dreading him ringing her door. Still, though, when it wasn't him ringing she was surprised at the way her heart dropped to her shoes.

Nicci knew she looked awful, her eyes red from crying and quickly she put some face powder on and mascara'd her lashes until she almost looked normal. That was always her all over, Nicci thought, bitterly — putting on a mask for the world, even for her best friend. She'd lied to people, pretended she could read when she couldn't, and this make-up, pretending everything was fine when it wasn't, was just another mask.

Nicci breathed deeply and opened the door. Cat was in a complete lather. At first Nicci thought it was something to do with Zippy but when Cat told her what Luke had been up to at the bank, Nicci was astonished. For a moment as they sat in Nicci's cosy lounge, Cat's problem made her forget her own considerable troubles.

'Can you believe it, Nicci, what that rat was going to do? And he was going to land me with the blame for everything. And to think I was falling for him? Grant Blake was so nice to me, he couldn't have been kinder.'

'We can all fall for people who turn out to be bad for us,' Nicci said bitterly, at the mention of Grant's name. How could she possibly face him again when he knew her awful secret? There he was, educated and successful, and there she was, stupid and as illiterate as a one year old.

She glanced over at her bookcase.

Yes, she loved books, in fact she collected old books, loved to run her hands over the gold lettering, loved to open them up and smell the musty pages and wonder what incredible knowledge they held inside them. Today, she'd go and sell all those beautiful books to the antique shop down the road. She might as well face facts. She was never going to be able to read them. That, like having her own shop, was just a pipe dream and she was no more than a fool.

Poor Cat, Nicci realised she should be comforting her friend, not thinking about herself. 'I'm so sorry for you Cat.'

'Do you know, I'm not. I thought Luke was special because he was good looking and he made me laugh, but actually I realise there's someone far more special.'

'You mean Dean?'

'Absolutely. Dean's not flashy and full of empty promises. If he makes a promise he keeps it. He's sweet and caring — and he's a great dancer,' she laughed. 'I don't know why I ever thought Luke was better. Now I realise I had a lucky escape. I think I'll ring Dean now and tell him everything that's happened and ask him to pick me up. I know he will.'

'Of course he will, he'll jump at it.'

'He'll even bring Zippy if I ask him. Zippy's okay by the way. Dean and I took him to the vet again and he just had a virus. All's well that ends well, so they say.'

'Absolutely.' Nicci had never felt so lonely than when she saw Cat go off to the bedroom to make a private, romantic phone call to Dean. She was delighted for her friend but it did throw her own solitude into relief.

'He'll be here in fifteen minutes.'

Nicci opened the door to Dean and was so pleased for Cat that she had someone special to confide in. She watched from the window as Dean put his arm around Cat to guide her across the road. Cat looked so happy, so complete. Tears swelled in Nicci's eyes as she went to the kitchen, took out a large carrier bag then went to the lounge and started to pull the books out of her bookcase, loading them into the bag. They were useless things, she couldn't even make out if they were the right way up. She was disgusted with herself.

When there came another ring at her door, Nicci, swiftly wiped away the tears, thinking must have forgotten something, maybe her mobile phone. But there was Grant, large as life, holding of all the ridiculous things, a file under his arm, as if he was an insurance salesman or something.

'Go away,' Nicci said rudely, pushing the door back against him, 'I've got nothing to say to you.'

Grant stood his ground, not letting her close the door. 'I know you only opened the door because you thought it was Cat. I . . . it was actually me who drove her here.'

'What?' Relenting a fraction, Nicci

opened the door wider. 'Go away, Grant please. There's nothing here for you.' Dishevelled, barefoot, her make-up streaked, pale faced and with dark rings under her eyes from lack of sleep, Nicci looked as wretched as she felt.

'But there is, Nicci, there's you.'

Nicci stared at Grant, her steely gaze full of suspicion. She had suspected him of coming here to laugh at her, to complain at her for wasting his time, asking for a loan when she couldn't be trusted even to read a contract or fill in a form. But, there was no mockery in his eyes, only care and compassion.

'I hope you don't feel sorry for me,' she stomped back into the room and he followed her. 'All my life I've been scared of people finding out and feeling sorry for me. I can make my own way, I don't need anyone else.'

'We all need someone,' said Grant. 'I'm beginning to find that out now.'

She stood, like a cornered animal, her books strewn over the floor, filling up the bag. Grant looked aghast, 'What are you doing to all your books?'

'What do you think I'm doing?' Her voice was hard with scorn. 'I'm throwing them out. I'll never need them.'

'Oh, I think you will.' Grant squared up to Nicci, almost daring her to contradict him.

'Don't mock me Grant. You know they're useless to me and they always will be.'

He bent down, picked one up and put it back in the bookcase. 'Great Expectations,' he mused, 'That's a wonderful book and just right for you because you have great expectations too. And what's more, I know you'll achieve them, every one.'

Nicci frowned at him, her tear streaked face taut and strained. 'You're talking in riddles, Grant. I wish you'd just go away and leave me alone.'

'No way.' He came to stand next to her, he took her hand. 'You're going to start working and if I have my way, before this year is out, you'll be reading

Great Expectations to me.'

Nicci wrenched her hand out of his. 'How could you make fun of me?'

'I'm not,' he grasped her again, with both hands this time and his look and his hold meant business. 'You're going to learn to read and I'm going to teach you.'

'What?'

'That's right. It's not impossible. Oh, it'll take time and effort on both our parts and there'll be laughter and tears I've no doubt in equal amounts. But we'll beat it — together. I know you can Nicci, you're so strong, so determined. Together we'll do it.'

A spark ignited her pretty features then died just as instantly. 'Forget it.'

'Why?'

'Don't you think I haven't tried? Don't you think I've been to classes, don't you think teachers have tried their hardest with me? I even went to evening classes as an adult. It was humiliating. I was the only one who didn't make it. I'm a lost cause.'

'I don't believe that Nicci and neither do you. There are ways, techniques. I've been reading up on them. I downloaded stuff from the web.'

'I never even learned my letters.'

'You can. There's one woman I read about, just like you. She had her own business, too, in fact. She ran a very successful cleaning contractors. For ages her teacher thought he couldn't get through to her, she just couldn't remember the letters like his other pupils did. Then, he had a brainwave, he shaped the letters for her in anything he could find — pipe cleaners, Blu-Tack . . . see? Just like this . . .'

Grant took a packet of Blu-Tack out of his pocket, placed a roll of it on the table, stretched and kneaded it and started fashioning it into a C. Nicci looked down amazed. She touched the shape, drew her fingers around the curve. No one had ever tried to teach her like that before. Once she felt the shape, she closed her eyes. She could picture it in the black recesses of her mind, just because she could feel it, she could now picture it.

'And here,' Grant, was going up a gear, smiling, almost laughing, 'See here, Nicci, here's an A. Feel it on the table, it's all straight lines, it looks just like a builder's stepladder.'

In disbelief, Nicci ran her fingers over the shape he had made. It came alive once her fingertips could touch it, the shape imprinted itself on her brain in a way she had never experienced before.

Grant was laughing now, a full throated, joyous sound. 'Try this one I've made here; it's a T, more straight lines.' He got her to say the sounds over and over as he lead her fingers over the shapes of the letters, 'A like in Apple, C like in cake, T like in tea!'

Nicci started laughing too. All the tension and upset she had always felt in the past when someone tried to teach her to read and failed, all the frustration had disappeared. There was nothing other than a slow realisation. It was like she was looking at a wave running away from a rock, revealing shapes and creatures lying in a rock pool, as clear as day. The letters and the sounds came clear to her.

'See?' smiled Grant, 'If I put them in this sequence, what do they spell?'

He placed the Blu-Tack letters in a line, one after the other and listened intently as Nicci said the sounds, 'C . . . A . . . T.' She beamed at him as she tentatively put the letters together into a word. 'Cat! It's Cat's name. And I read it on my own.'

'That's right.' He looked at her fondly her as he brought his arms round her and tenderly held her to him. 'You did it, Nicci. You did it yourself.'

And she knew he was right; he had shown her the way. How could she ever have hated him? How could she have distrusted him when all he wanted to do was to help?

'What's more,' he said, 'I had an email from head office today to say that the bank is releasing more funds. The loan's yours Nicci. The shop can be

189

yours. Everything you want can be yours, if you want it. Even . . . even me . . . That's if you want me, if you forgive me . . . '

She felt the warmth of his arms enfolding her with love. 'There's nothing to forgive,' she said and as she did so, she smelt the scent of his newly washed hair, the tinge of sandalwood aftershave. Gently she reached up and pulled him down to her. She wanted him so, so much.

When he kissed her, she couldn't hold him tightly enough, couldn't embrace him with more passion. Her knees felt weak and would have buckled under her if he hadn't lifted her, swept her up in the air and, as he kissed her, whirled her gently around making her dizzy with love and desire and total happiness. His lips against hers at first were tentative, as soft as a butterfly's wing, as delicious as champagne. Then, his need burnt with a passion that thrilled the very depths of her, which threatened to make her cry all over